JOIN THE FUN IN CABIN SIX . . .

KATIE is the perfect team player. She loves competitive games, planned activities, and coming up with her own great ideas.

MEGAN would rather lose herself in fantasyland than get into organized fun.

SARAH would be much happier if she could spend her time reading instead of exerting herself.

ERIN is much more interested in boys, clothes, and makeup than in playing kids' games at camp.

TRINA hates conflicts. She just wants everyone to be happy . . .

AND THEY ARE! Despite all their differences, the Cabin Six bunch are having the time of their lives at CAMP SUNNYSIDE!

Look for More Fun and Games with
CAMP SUNNYSIDE FRIENDS
by Marilyn Kaye
from Avon Books

(#1) NO BOYS ALLOWED!
(#2) CABIN SIX PLAYS CUPID
(#3) COLOR WAR!
(#4) NEW GIRL IN CABIN SIX
(#5) LOOKING FOR TROUBLE
(#6) KATIE STEALS THE SHOW
(#7) A WITCH IN CABIN SIX
(#8) TOO MANY COUNSELORS
(#9) THE NEW-AND-IMPROVED SARAH
(#10) ERIN AND THE MOVIE STAR
(#11) THE PROBLEM WITH PARENTS
(#12) THE TENNIS TRAP
(#13) BIG SISTER BLUES
(#14) MEGAN'S GHOST

And Don't Forget to Pick Up . . .

CAMP SUNNYSIDE FRIENDS SPECIAL: CHRISTMAS REUNION
MY CAMP MEMORY BOOK

Coming Soon

(#16) HAPPILY EVER AFTER

MARILYN KAYE is the author of many popular books for young readers, including the "Out of This World" series and the "Sisters" books. She is an associate professor at St. John's University and lives in Brooklyn, New York. Camp Sunnyside is the camp Marilyn Kaye wishes that she had gone to every summer when she was a kid.

Avon Books are available at special quantity discounts for bulk purchases for sales promotions, premiums, fund raising or educational use. Special books, or book excerpts, can also be created to fit specific needs.

For details write or telephone the office of the Director of Special Markets, Avon Books, Dept. FP, 1350 Avenue of the Americas, New York, New York 10019, 1-800-238-0658.

Christmas Break

Marilyn Kaye

If you purchased this book without a cover, you should be aware that this book is stolen property. It was reported as "unsold and destroyed" to the publisher, and neither the author nor the publisher has received any payment for this "stripped book."

CAMP SUNNYSIDE FRIENDS #15: CHRISTMAS BREAK is an original publication of Avon Books. This work has never before appeared in book form.

AVON BOOKS
A division of
The Hearst Corporation
1350 Avenue of the Americas
New York, New York 10019

Copyright © 1991 by Marilyn Kaye
Published by arrangement with the author
Library of Congress Catalog Card Number: 91-92080
ISBN: 0-380-76553-5
RL: 4.9

All rights reserved, which includes the right to reproduce this book or portions thereof in any form whatsoever except as provided by the U.S. Copyright Law. For information address Writers House Inc., 21 West 26th Street, New York, New York 10010.

First Avon Camelot Printing: December 1991

CAMELOT TRADEMARK REG. U.S. PAT. OFF. AND IN OTHER COUNTRIES, MARCA REGISTRADA, HECHO EN U.S.A.

Printed in the U.S.A.

OPM 10 9 8 7 6 5 4 3 2 1

For Jacki Marino

Christmas Break

Chapter 1

"Deck the halls with boughs of holly," Katie Dillon sang softly as she hurried home from school one December afternoon. It was so cold she could see her own breath, and she almost slipped a few times on icy sidewalk patches. The wind seemed to bite right through the scarf wrapped around her neck, and Kate shivered. But she went right on singing. She was in such a good mood nothing could bother her.

If it wasn't for the winter weather, she would have thought this was June from the way she was feeling. When school let out for summer vacation, she always found herself singing on the way home from school. It was usually a Camp Sunnyside song, since that was what she'd be thinking about. That day in June was always a happy one, with three months away from school and camp to look forward to.

But today, school was over until after New Year's, and that felt almost as good. Especially because the Dillon family had special plans for this vacation.

She quickened her pace as she approached her house. "I'm home!" she yelled, walking in the door. She pulled off her coat, scarf, and hat and tossed them on the coatrack.

"I'm in here," a voice floated out from the kitchen.

Katie was happy to hear the response. Her mother taught classes at the junior college and often wasn't home when Katie returned from school. When she *was* home, Katie appreciated having her mother's undivided attention, before her twin brothers and her father came home.

"Hi, Mom," she sang out as she entered the kitchen.

Her mother greeted her with a smile. "You certainly look happy."

"Of course I'm happy! School's out for three whole weeks. Christmas is just around the corner. And after Christmas"—she hugged herself with glee—"Holly Hills!"

"I'm looking forward to this holiday too," Mrs. Dillon said. "I just hope I remember how to ski."

"Don't worry," Katie assured her. "I think it's like bicycle riding. You never really forget how to do it. Once you've got those skis on your feet and the poles in your hands, it will come right back to you."

Her mother laughed. "You've become quite an authority on the subject!" She handed Katie a glass of milk and plunked the cookie jar on the table.

Katie took a cookie and bit into it. "I haven't been able to think about anything else since Dad told us we're going back to Holly Hills." In her mind, she could see herself sailing down a hill. She could hear the wind rushing past her, she could feel the soft satin of the snow as she glided along. "Do you think I can ski alone on the intermediate slopes this year?"

"We'll let the ski instructor decide that," Mrs. Dillon said. "He'll be able to evaluate you."

"I'm eleven now," Katie pointed out. "Peter and Michael were skiing on the intermediate slopes when they were eleven."

"It's not your age that matters," her mother countered. "It's your ability to handle the slope."

"I'm too big for the beginner slope," Katie persisted. "And I don't want to be in ski-wee again."

"Ski-wee?"

"You know, ski school with a bunch of little kids."

"Katie, I promise you, we'll have the instructor watch you on the beginner slope. And if he or she thinks you're ready, you can move up." Her tone made it clear that this was the last word on the subject. "Now, let's think about what you're going to need."

As her mother began to talk about clothes, Katie let her thoughts drift. Wouldn't it be something if the ski instructor thought she had improved dramatically since last year? Maybe she could move right on to the advanced slopes her twin brothers were skiing on!

"Katie, are you listening to me?"

"Huh? Oh, sure, Mom."

"Then go on up to your room and see if your ski pants still fit."

"Okay." Grabbing another cookie, Katie

ran upstairs. Entering her room, she caught a glimpse of herself in the mirror. There was a wicked glint in her eyes, and she knew what had put it there. It was the thought of shocking her brothers by showing up on the same slope as them.

It seemed like all her life, they were ahead of her. They were always bigger, they had later bedtimes, they got to do things she wasn't allowed to do. Of course, there wasn't much she could do about that, and it wasn't really their fault. After all, they were two years older.

And they never let her forget that. They were always teasing her, showing off, and pointing out all the ways they were superior to her. It would be so super to catch up with them once in a while. On the ski slope, she had a chance to do that. Last year, the ski instructor told her she had a natural talent for skiing. She fervently hoped the same instructor would be at Holly Hills this year.

Recalling her mother's instructions, she went to the dresser and rummaged through a drawer till she found a pair of red ski pants. Quickly, she undressed and tried them on.

She could feel that they were uncomfortably tight. But even so, seeing her reflection in the mirror made her feel giddy. She bent her knees, arched her back, and went into a skiing pose.

Katie loved lots of sports, but skiing was special. There was the sense of anticipation as she rode up the hill on the lift. Then there was the excitement of standing poised at the top, clutching the poles. And then there was the ultimate sensation, pushing off, picking up speed—it was like flying!

She snatched the photo album from her desk and began flipping through it, looking for pictures that would remind her of Holly Hills. As usual, though, like every other time she went through the album looking for a particular picture, other photos distracted her and grabbed her attention.

Like all those Camp Sunnyside pictures . . . there was one that she loved, because it showed all the cabin six girls together. And each of them looked exactly the way she always pictured them in her mind.

In the photo, they were sitting on the grass, watching a softball game. She herself was right up front, with her mouth open and a fist raised in the air. Katie couldn't tell if she was cheering the Sunnyside team or booing the Camp Eagle team. Her best camp friend, Trina, sat next to her, smiling brightly. Little redheaded Megan wasn't even watching the game, and the glazed expression on her face meant she was daydreaming. Sarah's head was down, and even though it couldn't be seen in the picture, Katie knew there was an open book on Sarah's lap. Erin was looking off to the side, with the annoying smile that meant a cute boy was within her viewing range.

Katie wondered what they were all doing for the holidays, and she reminded herself to write out Christmas cards to the gang that evening. Then she turned the page and found some pictures from her last trip to Holly Hills.

There she was, all decked out in her ski clothes, standing in front of the lodge. And there was another of her, waiting for the lift.

Something occurred to her as she examined the pictures. Except for the occasional snapshot with her parents, in every one she was alone.

That wasn't surprising, really. As soon as they'd arrived at Holly Hills, her brothers had hooked up with a couple of guys, and they were barely to be seen the rest of the week. Her parents had made friends too.

Katie had been by herself. Well, not all the time. She ate meals with her parents. But there weren't any other kids around that Katie could have hung out with. There were lots of teenagers, and some really little kids. But not one girl Katie's age, or even close.

Memories flooded back. She saw herself, standing alone in the midst of little kids in ski-wee. Sitting in the lounge, flipping through comic books. Watching boring reruns on the television in her room.

Funny, how she'd forgotten about all that. What stuck in her mind was the thrill of skiing. The boredom and loneliness when she wasn't on the slopes had faded from her memory.

But these photos brought it all back. She'd become so desperate for companionship she'd even made a stab at tagging along with her brothers. It wasn't very satisfying. The boys either ignored her or teased her.

Suddenly, she wasn't quite as excited as she'd been just minutes ago. She was still looking forward to the skiing. But the thought of those endless hours alone in the evening wasn't exactly appealing.

Lost in her thoughts, she jumped when she heard her mother's voice. "Well? Do they fit?"

Katie blinked. "Huh?"

"Your ski pants from last year. Can you still wear them?"

Obediently, Katie rose and presented herself. Her mother sighed as she examined Katie's appearance. "You *have* grown. It looks like we'll have to do a little shopping before we go."

"Yeah, okay."

Her mother cocked her head thoughtfully. "I know shopping for clothes isn't one of your absolutely favorite activities, but you can't ski naked!"

Katie worked up a halfhearted smile. "No, I guess not."

It was impossible to hide anything from her mother. "Is something wrong? Just five minutes ago you were bouncing all over the house."

Katie shrugged. "It's just that . . . well, I was thinking about the last time we went to Holly Hills."

"But you had a wonderful time there, didn't you?"

Katie nodded. "When I was skiing. But there were no other kids there to hang around with. I was always alone."

Slowly, Mrs. Dillon nodded. "Yes, I remember that. You never complained, though."

"There was nothing anyone could do about it," Katie replied. "Besides, if I'd started complaining, you might have made Peter and Michael drag me around with them!"

Her mother's lips twitched. "I suppose there are fates worse than being alone. Well, maybe there will be someone your age there this year. Of course, I can't guarantee that, but . . ." She paused. "Actually, there *is* a way to guarantee that."

"How?" Katie asked.

"You could invite a friend to go with us."

Katie gasped. "Mom! Could I?"

"Why not? Your room at the lodge will have two beds. It's a shame to waste one."

Katie began to pace the room. "Who should I ask? Courtney's going to her grandparents' for the holidays. Jennifer's sister is coming home from college, so she won't want to leave. I think Emily's got relatives visiting her too."

"I've got an idea," Mrs. Dillon said. "Why not ask one of your Sunnyside friends to join us?"

Katie gasped again. "Mom, that's brilliant!"

Her mother started talking about shopping tomorrow, but Katie wasn't really listening. Her spirits were soaring. Now she could have the perfect holiday. A week on the slopes of Holly Hills—and a friend to share it all with!

Five minutes after the last school bell rang, Erin Chapman was sliding into a booth at the Sweet Shoppe, an ice-cream parlor just across the street from Miss Harrington's School for Girls. The friend sitting across from her wore the same outfit Erin wore—a navy blue skirt with a matching blazer. Practically every girl in the Sweet Shoppe wore identical clothes. It was the Harrington uniform.

"What are you frowning about?" Marcia asked.

Erin took a sip of her diet soda. "I was just thinking how boring these uniforms are." She adjusted the scarf around her neck. She and her friends usually tried to add something to make their look unique. Erin wore scarves.

Marcia always had a cute little pin affixed to her lapel.

"Think about this," Marcia advised. "We don't have to wear these uniforms again for three weeks!"

Two other identically dressed girls joined them in the booth. Hilary had an embroidered vest under the blazer, and Claire had rolled her skirt up to way above her knees.

"Well, I've just decided what I want for Christmas," Hilary announced.

"What?" Erin asked.

Hilary turned her head and nodded toward a corner of the restaurant. "That."

They all turned to look at the waiter taking someone's order.

"Take a good look," Hilary continued. "He's gorgeous."

Claire giggled. "I wouldn't mind finding some really cute guy gift-wrapped under the Christmas tree."

"Who needs gift wrapping?" Marcia joked.

Erin rolled her eyes. "He's not all that cute, Hilary. He just looks great because he's the only boy within a mile of this place." It was the major drawback of an all-girls school.

"Oh, well," Hilary sighed. "I guess I'll have

to be satisfied with what I know I *am* getting for Christmas." She paused, and smiled secretively.

"Okay, cut the drama," Marcia ordered. "What are you getting?"

"An *intense* shopping spree. In New York! My grandmother's taking me, and she says there's absolutely no limit to what I can get."

The other girls looked suitably impressed. Personally, Erin thought Hilary was probably exaggerating, but she didn't challenge her. She'd get around to topping Hilary soon enough.

"My parents never know what to give me," Claire said. "Usually I get a gift certificate, which is fine with me."

"But that's not very Christmassy," Marcia objected. "My parents like to give me real presents." She grinned. "And then I take them back to the stores and exchange them for what I really want."

Erin was dying to break her news to them. But she wanted to wait for the perfect moment. Still, it wouldn't hurt to get the conversation going in the right direction. "Are you guys staying in town for the holidays?"

"Yeah," Marcia said.

"We're going to my grandparents' in Ohio," Claire told them.

"What about you?" Hilary asked.

It was the right moment. Erin studied her fingernails casually. "My father has to go to some meeting in Texas, right after Christmas day. So my mother and I are going to a spa in California."

"A what?" Claire asked.

"You know, a spa. A beauty resort."

She got the reaction she'd hoped for. Eyes widened, mouths dropped open. There was unconcealed admiration on every face.

"Wow! Lucky you!" Marcia exclaimed.

Erin smiled and nodded. "I think it's going to be nice. I'll have facials every day, manicures and pedicures. Oh, yeah . . ." she paused. "I'll be getting a total makeover too."

This brought cries of envy from her classmates. "That is *so* neat!" Hilary squealed.

"You guys might not even recognize me when I get back," Erin said. She gathered her long blonde hair and lifted it off her neck. "How do you think I'd look with a short curly perm?"

An hour later, at home, Erin was still enjoying the memory of her friends' reaction.

Going to a spa—that was definitely an unusual place to go for the holidays. Her mother planned to diet and exercise and lose five pounds. Erin planned to take advantage of every possible beauty treatment, and spend the rest of the time at the pool, getting a fantastic tan.

She felt glamorous just thinking about it. She decided to go through her clothes and start picking out what she'd take.

As she went to the dresser, she noticed that an envelope had been left there for her. Opening it, she saw that it was a Christmas card from Megan. As she read the short note inside, her thoughts went back to another winter holiday.

It was just a year ago that the cabin six girls had gathered for a reunion at Katie's. And it was fun, Erin remembered. But definitely not as exciting as going to a real beauty spa. She'd have to send her Camp Sunnyside friends postcards from the place. Of course, they probably wouldn't appreciate the importance of going to a spa. The Sunnyside girls were neat, in their way. But they weren't very sophisticated.

Glancing out the window, she noticed a

light snow starting to fall. It was amazing to think that in one week, she'd be wearing a bikini!

There was a light rap on the door.

"Come in!"

Erin's mother stood there. "Hello, dear. How was school?"

"Same as always," Erin said. "Mother, do you think I could get a new bathing suit for our trip?"

Mrs. Chapman was silent for a minute. "Erin, I need to talk with you about that." She smiled, but it wasn't a happy smile. It was more like a sympathetic one.

A cold shiver went up Erin's back. She had the uneasy feeling bad news was coming.

She was right.

"Your father wants me to go with him to that meeting in Texas after Christmas."

Erin stared at her in dismay. "But what about the spa?"

There was sincere regret on her mother's face. "I'm sorry, dear. We'll have to put that off. Of course, you can go with us to Texas."

"But what will I do in Texas?" Erin wailed.

"I know; it wouldn't be much fun for you," Mrs. Chapman agreed. "Would you like to visit Aunt Linda in Connecticut? Or maybe you'd prefer to stay with one of your friends here. We'll talk about it later. I am truly sorry, Erin."

Erin could tell her mother really felt awful about this. But she couldn't feel nearly as awful as Erin felt. As soon as her mother left, she threw herself on her bed.

How was she going to face her friends?

Chapter 2

Katie sauntered into the kitchen, with Peter and Michael close behind. With outrage, the twins confronted their mother.

"Did you tell Katie she could invite a friend to go with us to Holly Hills?" Peter demanded.

Mrs. Dillon glanced up from the stack of college essays she was grading and nodded.

"Then we can invite someone too?" Michael asked. Mrs. Dillon shook her head and went back to grading.

Katie beamed. It seemed like just the other day *she* was asking, Why do Peter and Michael get to stay up late and I don't? Now the shoe was on the other foot—and it felt like a perfect fit!

Peter folded his arms across his chest.

"Why does Katie get to invite a friend and we don't? It's not fair!"

"Not fair at all!" Michael echoed.

Mrs. Dillon didn't even bother to raise her eyes from the essays. "Now, boys, don't fuss."

Peter scowled. "I don't get it."

His identical twin wore an identical expression. "Yeah. Why is *she* getting special privileges?"

Their mother looked up. "Look, you two have each other to pal around with at Holly Hills. Katie deserves to have someone too. And I don't want to hear another word of complaint about it. *Now* do you get it?"

Neither of the boys looked pleased with her explanation. But they knew better than to continue the argument. With a grunt and a sullen expression, Peter ambled over to the refrigerator, while Michael dug his hand into the cookie jar.

Katie was enjoying every minute of this. "Thanks, Mom."

"Katie, have you decided who you're going to invite?" her mother asked.

Katie nodded happily. "Trina. I tried calling her but the line was busy. I'm going to try again in a few minutes."

Peter turned away from his examination of the contents of the refrigerator and gazed at his sister with interest. "Trina. Is she the pretty one with long blonde hair?"

"No, that's Erin."

"Why don't you invite *her?*" Michael suggested.

"No way," Katie stated. A vision of Erin flashed through her head. Erin was okay, in her own way. At Sunnyside, the other girls were used to the way she constantly primped, bragged, talked about boys, and nagged her cabin mates to improve their appearances. It didn't really bother them, and sometimes it was even fun to listen to her.

But Katie recalled that Sunnyside Christmas reunion, when Erin spent more time trying to flirt with Peter and Michael than she spent with her own friends. No, Erin was the last person Katie would want as a companion at Holly Hills.

Peter turned to their mother. "Can't we at least have some say about who Katie brings?"

"Nope," she replied. "It's Katie's decision."

Michael sighed in resignation. "At least if Katie's got one of her little friends there, she won't try to tag along with us again."

Katie didn't know which part of that remark was more insulting—calling Trina "a little friend" or that remark about tagging along. But she didn't want to start any arguments in front of their mother. "I'm going to try Trina's number again. Mom, can I use the phone in your bedroom?"

Getting permission, Katie left the kitchen. Unfortunately, her brothers followed her upstairs. Katie tried to ignore their conversation, but they spoke to each other loudly—probably just to make sure she could hear.

"Katie can't tag along with us anyway," Peter said. "It's not like we'll be skiing the same slopes."

Katie couldn't resist. "That's how much *you* know. I'll be on the advanced slopes with you by the second day."

The look of dismay she'd hoped to see on their faces didn't appear. Instead, she got a chorus of laughter. "That'll be the day. You'll be lucky to get out of ski-wee!" Michael hooted.

As the two of them sauntered into their room, Katie clenched her teeth. She should have known they wouldn't take her seriously. She comforted herself with imagining the looks on their faces when she showed up on the advanced slopes.

Anyway, she had more important things on her mind. She went into her parents' bedroom and shut the door.

She dialed the number and settled back on the bed as it began ringing. Trina herself answered. "Hello?"

"Trina, guess who?"

"Katie!" Trina wasn't someone who screamed with excitement, but Katie could hear the pleasure in her voice. "I'm so happy to hear from you!"

"You're going to be even happier when I tell you why I called," Katie said.

"Are you having another Sunnyside reunion?"

"No, better. We're going skiing at Holly Hills."

"Lucky you," Trina said. "You're going to have a great time."

"Don't say you, say us. You and me! My mother said I could invite a friend to come with us!"

"And you're inviting me?"

"You got it! Oh, Trina, we're going to have so much fun!"

There was a silence at the other end. Katie wondered if they'd been disconnected. "Trina? Are you there?"

"I'm here." But there wasn't any excitement in her voice. "Oh, Katie, I wish I could come. But Sarah's spending the week between Christmas and New Year's here. See, her father's going to a medical conference, and her sister's visiting friends. So I invited her to come here."

Katie couldn't say the news was a big surprise. Ms. Sandburg, Trina's mother, was divorced. Dr. Fine, Sarah's father, was widowed. They'd met while visiting their daughters at Camp Sunnyside, and they'd become good friends. According to Trina's letters, the two families got together frequently.

"Katie? Are you there?"

"Yeah. Look, maybe my parents would let me take two friends."

"That would be neat," Trina said. "But you know how Sarah is about sports. She wouldn't want to go skiing."

"But we got her to start swimming at Sunnyside. Maybe you could convince her to try skiing."

"Well, I'll try," Trina said. "But I doubt I'd be able to talk her into it."

"Darn," Katie muttered.

"Yeah," Trina agreed. "I mean, it'll be neat having a holiday with Sarah, but . . . you know."

Katie knew. While Trina and Sarah were friends, Trina and Katie were *best* friends.

"I guess I'll invite Megan," Katie said.

"Lucky Megan," Trina said.

They hung up with promises to talk again soon. Katie went to her room and got her address book. As she came back out, Michael emerged from his room.

"Did you invite your little friend?" he asked in that disgusting, I'm-so-superior-to-you voice.

"She can't come," Katie said.

Michael looked hopeful. "Then how about inviting that Erin?"

"Forget it," Katie snapped, and went back into her parents' bedroom. She sat down on the bed and dialed the number.

"Megan, hi, it's Katie."

This time she got an excited squeal. "Katie! Hi! What's new?"

Katie went right to the point. "My family's going skiing after Christmas, and—"

Megan interrupted. "Ooh, you're so lucky!"

"*We're* lucky!" Katie announced. "My parents say I can invite a friend to come with us, so—"

Again, Megan broke in. "Oh no!"

It wasn't the reaction Katie had anticipated. "What do you mean, oh no?"

"I'm grounded," Megan wailed. "I got a bad progress report for my English class."

"Oh, Megan," Katie moaned. "Are you sure you can't talk your parents out of being grounded?"

"I don't dare even ask," Megan replied. She sounded just as depressed as Katie did.

When she hung up the phone, Katie stared at it glumly. There was only one cabin six girl left to call. And she was the only one Katie didn't want to ask.

Erin would be absolutely no fun at all. She'd be more concerned with how she looked in ski clothes than how she skied. She'd ignore Katie to flirt with Peter and Michael. And she'd criticize everything Katie did.

But anything was better than being alone.

* * *

Erin lay flat on her bed and stared up at the ceiling. Beside her bed, the phone rang, but she didn't answer it. She let her answering machine take it.

The machine clicked on at the third ring. She couldn't avoid hearing the message. "Erin, it's Hilary. I'm thinking about having a party New Year's. When are you getting back from the spa? Call me."

Erin groaned. Oh, how she dreaded telling them all that her vacation plans were canceled. They'd all be sympathetic, but Erin didn't want their pity. Maybe they'd think she'd made up the story to begin with. That would be even worse.

For a few seconds, she contemplated pretending she had gone. She'd read enough about health spas in fashion magazines to make a convincing story of her experience.

But no, that wouldn't work. She'd have to hide from everyone for a whole week. And she had to arrange to stay with one of her friends anyway.

This was all just too, too awful. She winced as the phone started ringing again.

"Uh, hello, Erin, this is Katie. Katie Dillon."

Erin reached over and snatched up the phone. "Hi, Katie."

"You're there!"

"Yeah, sometimes I just leave the machine on even when I'm home. You know, in case some boy's calling who I don't want to talk to."

"Oh, right. Listen, how would you like to go skiing in the week between Christmas and New Year's?"

Erin listened as Katie described the plans. Her spirits lifted. A ski resort! That was almost as good as a health spa.

"Well, of course, I've already got other plans," she began. "This is awfully short notice, Katie."

"Yeah, I figured you might already have made plans for the holidays. I understand. It's too bad you can't come, but—"

"Wait," Erin said quickly. "What I was about to say is that I just might be able to change my plans to come with you. I love to ski, and I haven't seen you in ages. . . ."

"Okay," Katie said. She didn't sound particularly thrilled with the fact that Erin had accepted, but Erin didn't care.

"My mom will want to talk to your mom," Katie continued.

"She's not home right now. I'll tell her to call your mother tonight," Erin replied.

Hanging up, Erin raced to the closet. Where had she put that fantastic ski outfit she bought the month before?

This is great, she thought happily as she rummaged through her clothes. She'd only been skiing twice before in her life, and she wasn't very good at it. But who cared?

She snatched up a magazine she'd left on her bed. It had a whole article about ski resorts. She ignored the pictures of people skiing down hills and focused on another page. The headline read "Après-ski." She knew what that meant. It was French for what you did after skiing.

The photo showed some really cute guys with some girls, gathered in big cozy chairs around a blazing fire. Erin smiled happily. It wasn't the snow and the slopes she was looking forward to.

Après-ski! *That* was her style!

Katie dragged herself off the bed, made a swipe at straightening the wrinkles on the bedspread, and went downstairs.

In the kitchen, her mother was gathering the papers off the table. "Katie, would you set the table for dinner, please?"

"Okay."

Her tone caught her mother's attention. "What's wrong now?"

"Trina can't come to Holly Hills. Sarah's staying with her that week. Megan can't come, because she's grounded. So I called Erin."

"And she can't come either?"

"No, she's coming. Her mother's going to call you later."

"Then what's the problem?" Mrs. Dillon asked.

"I just would have rather had one of the others."

"I'm sure you and Erin will have lots of fun," her mother said.

"Maybe," Katie replied. But she was already beginning to wonder if being alone would have been so bad. Just then the phone rang, and Katie grabbed it.

"Hello?"

"Katie, it's Megan. Guess what!" Her voice was bubbling with excitement. "They said yes!"

"What?"

"My parents! I begged and begged, and promised I'd study like mad from now on. And they said I could go skiing with you!"

Katie let out a cheer. "Megan, that's super!"

"My mother wants to talk to your mother," Megan said. "Hold on."

Katie turned to *her* mother. "Mom, Megan can come after all!"

"But you've already asked Erin," Mrs. Dillon said.

"I'll just call her and take back the invitation."

Mrs. Dillon folded her arms across her chest. "Oh no you won't, young lady. That's incredibly rude and thoughtless and totally wrong."

"But, Mom, I know I'd have so much more fun with Megan! *Please?*"

Her mother's lips tightened. Katie knew what that meant. There was no point in asking that again. So she asked something else.

"Then could Megan come too?" Katie begged. On the phone, she heard Megan's mother say, "Hello?"

"Uh, hello, Mrs. Lindsay," Katie said. "Just

a minute." She held the phone toward her mother. Her mother gave her a sharp look, but she took it.

"Hello? Yes, well . . . not at all, we'd love to have Megan with us. Yes, fine."

Katie hugged herself in rapture as her mother talked to Mrs. Lindsay. And when Mrs. Dillon hung up the telephone, Katie hugged *her*. "Oh, Mom, thank you! You're the best mom in the whole wide world!"

When she looked up, she was relieved to see her mother was smiling. "Well, I couldn't exactly tell Mrs. Lindsay we were taking back our invitation, could I? Now, finish setting the table."

Mrs. Dillon left the kitchen. Katie hummed as she put plates down. With Megan there, she wouldn't care if Erin spent the week chasing after boys.

The phone rang again, and she got it. "Hello?"

"Katie, it's Trina. You're not going to believe this!"

"Believe what?"

"I just spoke to Sarah. And I talked her into going skiing!"

Katie gulped.

"Katie. Are you there?"

"Yeah, I'm here. Trina, that's—that's great!"

"Of course, my mother wants to talk to your mother."

"Right. Um, she's not here right now. I'll tell her to call when she gets back."

Hanging up, she sank down into a chair. On one hand, this was fabulous. It would be a real Sunnyside reunion! On the other hand—would her parents go for it?

Her mother returned. "Who was that?"

"Trina. Uh, Mom . . ."

Her mother closed her eyes for a minute. "Don't tell me. Now she can go too."

"And Sarah."

Now her mother sank into a chair. "Oh, Katie. *Five* girls to watch out for? That's an awfully big responsibility for your father and me."

"Mom, we're eleven years old! We can take care of ourselves! Honestly, we won't get into any trouble. We all know how to ski." Under her breath, she added, "Except Sarah. And it would be so wonderful to have all of cabin six there! Oh, Mom, please say yes!"

"I don't know what your father will say," Mrs. Dillon murmured.

"You won't even know we're there," Katie said. "Mom, if you say yes, I promise, I'll never ask for anything ever again."

Mrs. Dillon's lips twitched. "Can I get that in writing?"

"Huh?"

"Never mind." She shook her head wearily. And then she smiled and rose.

"What's Trina's number?"

Chapter 3

"Hey, quit shoving me!" Katie yelped.

"Why don't you move over?" Michael growled.

"There's no place to move to," Katie snapped back.

From the front seat of the car, their father declared, "If I hear one more complaint out of you kids, I'm turning this car around."

It wasn't a very believable threat, but Katie clamped her mouth shut anyway. She decided she'd limit her conversations with the twins to occasional nasty looks.

Besides, she really wasn't in the mood for arguing. She was too happy thinking about what lay ahead.

It was amazing, even miraculous, how perfectly everything had turned out! Not only was she on her way to a fabulous ski vacation, she'd have all her cabin six buddies to share it with. What more could any girl ask for?

Next to her, Michael shifted position and managed to land his elbow in her side. Katie squirmed around and tried to make herself more comfortable.

They wouldn't be so tightly crammed together like this if one of the girls had decided to make the trip with them. Then her father would have taken the station wagon. But the lodge wasn't far from where Sarah's father's conference was, so he was bringing Sarah and Trina, and they were picking Megan up on the way. Erin had called last night to say she'd meet them at the lodge.

Mrs. Dillon had said that was very thoughtful of Erin, since Erin's home was in the opposite direction of the lodge. Katie's father was pleased too, since he preferred to drive the smaller car.

Katie figured she knew the real reason Erin had decided she'd come to Holly Hills this way. She wanted to make a fancy entrance. Katie remembered Erin's arrivals at Sunnyside every summer. She was the only girl who was brought to the camp in a limousine, driven by a chauffeur.

She glanced over at her brothers. They were occupied, playing some portable electronic game. Katie yawned. Her father always made them leave for long trips early in the morning to beat the traffic. The sun wasn't even completely up yet, and it felt like night.

She slipped a headset over her ears and turned on her Walkman. Then she closed her eyes, and conjured up images of cabin six on the slopes.

She could see them all now, shrieking as they caught the lift up the hill, lining up side by side at the top. Maybe they'd have races. There she was, in the lead. Trina was close behind. Katie swerved to the left, then to the right. . . . She could see the judges waiting at the bottom. Just a few more yards and she'd have it—the Olympic gold medal!

But—oh no! She hit a bump! Then another bump! They were slowing her down!

With a start, Katie opened her eyes, and heard her father grumble, "There shouldn't be potholes like these on a highway."

"Now, dear, don't get upset," Mrs. Dillon murmured. She turned around and smiled at Katie. "Did you have a nice nap?"

Still feeling a little dazed, Katie rubbed her eyes. "How long was I asleep?"

"Three hours," her mother said. "We're almost there! Boys, wake up."

The bodies slumped together next to Katie didn't stir. "I'll take care of them," Katie said. She shoved her elbow into the side of the closest twin.

"Ow!" Michael's outraged cry woke Peter.

"Sorry," Katie said sweetly.

Her mother gave her one reproving look, and then exclaimed, "Look!"

Katie leaned forward. There were the mountains. A shiver of excitement sent tingles up and down her spine.

They passed some small cottages, and then they were pulling up in front of the lodge. As the family piled out, a young man hurried forward to help them with their luggage.

The lodge looked just like it did last year. She could see the cafeteria, and a huge living room with a gigantic fireplace. People strolled through the lodge, most of them carrying skis over their shoulders.

Her father was speaking to a man behind a reception desk. "The Dillon family. We have reservations."

"Here are the keys," the man said. "That's chalet number two and chalet number six."

Katie remembered that at ski resorts the cottages were called chalets. The man behind the desk spoke to her. "Chalet six is to the left of the lodge as you walk out. I believe some of your friends have already arrived."

Katie snatched up her suitcase, cried, "See ya later," and headed toward the door. Behind her, she heard her father say, "I think that will be the last time we'll be seeing her this week."

As she walked rapidly, Katie looked at the number on the key. Chalet 6. She grinned. That would be easy to remember! From cabin mates to chalet mates, she thought.

There were numbers on the doors of the little chalets. She passed numbers nine, eight, and seven, and practically ran up the walkway to number six. Just as she arrived at the door, it flew open.

"Katie!"

"Trina!"

The girls threw their arms around each other and jumped up and down. Sarah and Megan jumped in and made it a four-way hug.

"We told the man in the lodge to call us the

minute you arrived," Sarah said. "We were going to meet you halfway."

"Guess I was too fast for you guys," Katie declared.

"Did you see those mountains?" Megan squealed. "I can't wait!"

"*I* can," Sarah said. "They're so *big!*" She gave the others an abashed look. "I've never been on skis before."

They weren't surprised. "Don't worry," Megan said. "It's sort of like swimming, except standing up."

"And on snow, instead of in water," Trina added.

"And you don't wear a bathing suit," Katie put in.

Sarah rolled her eyes. "It doesn't sound like swimming at all."

Katie patted her arm. "It's not that hard. And the instructor will teach you." She looked around. "Gee, check out this place. It's *fancy.*"

The room they were in was like a living room, with a sofa, chairs, and a big television. "There are two bedrooms," Trina said. "Each has two beds."

"Great!" Katie said. "Who's going to sleep where?"

"Let's do it like camp," Megan suggested. "Me and Sarah together, and you guys together."

"What about Erin?" Trina asked.

"She can sleep on the sofa," Katie said.

Trina's forehead puckered. "I don't know if she'll like that."

Megan looked in one bedroom, and then in the other. "Hey, there are two bathrooms too!"

"You know what that will mean," Katie said. "One for Erin, and one for the rest of us!"

Sarah was examining the sofa. "I think this pulls out into a bed. It'll be twice the size of the beds in the bedrooms. And Erin will have this whole living room as her personal bedroom. That should make her happy."

Katie frowned. "Why are you all so worried about making Erin happy?"

"Because we don't want to listen to her complain," Megan promptly responded.

"Well, *I'm* going to start complaining if we don't get out on those slopes," Katie stated. "C'mon, you guys, let's get ready to go."

It didn't take long before they were all decked out in ski wear, with scarves and goggles hanging from their necks. "Let's go," Katie said.

Trina hesitated. "Don't you think we should wait for Erin?"

Katie sighed, and slumped down into a chair. "Yeah, I guess it wouldn't be very nice for us to leave before she gets here."

Megan turned on the TV, and they all stared at it for a few minutes. But everyone was getting restless.

"Where *is* she?" Katie complained. Just then, there was a knock on the door. Katie leaped up. "Finally." But when she opened the door, she found herself face-to-face with her brothers.

"What do *you* want?" she demanded. Then she noticed that they were both carrying suitcases. They brushed past her with them. And standing right behind them was Erin.

"Hi, everyone! Thanks, you guys."

While the others were greeting Erin, Katie was still recovering from the shock of seeing her brothers carrying someone else's suitcases. The boys suddenly became aware that she was staring at them, and they looked uncomfortable. "Uh, see ya," they mumbled, and hurried out.

"How much did you have to bribe them to carry your bags?" Katie asked Erin.

Erin leaned forward and kissed the air beside Katie's cheek. "Don't be silly. They're so sweet." She looked around. "This isn't bad."

"Hurry up and get dressed so we can go to the slopes," Katie urged.

"Two bags," Megan whispered to Katie in awe. "What does she think she needs to ski?" Erin rummaged through one of them and pulled out a hot pink ski outfit.

"Do you think I should wear this one? Or this one?" An identical outfit in turquoise came out.

"They're both very cute," Trina said.

"What does it matter?" Katie asked impatiently. "Just hurry up!"

"All right, all right." Erin hurried into one of the bedrooms, and the girls returned to the television. But after several minutes went by, Megan started to fidget.

"What's taking her so long?"

"Erin, come on!" Katie yelled.

"Just a minute," Erin called back. "I have to finish my makeup."

"Makeup!" Trina looked puzzled. And when Erin finally emerged, she asked, "Erin, why are you bothering with makeup? You'll have goggles on, and a scarf."

"But I'll have to take them off eventually, won't I?" She preened. "How do I look?"

Katie had to admit that Erin looked like a model demonstrating the latest in fashion ski wear. But she wasn't going to give her the satisfaction of telling her. "Come on, we have to rent our equipment and get to the slopes. I just hope the lift lines aren't horrendous."

After they got fitted out with boots, skis, and poles, the girls made their way toward the trails.

"How are you supposed to lift your feet in these things?" Sarah asked.

Megan giggled. "You're supposed to glide, silly."

With an expression of grim determination, Sarah pushed herself forward.

"Not that way," Katie called out. "That's the wrong trail."

"How can you tell?" Sarah asked.

"See that sign? It's got a black diamond on it. That means this trail leads to an expert slope."

Sarah slid backward very quickly. "I definitely don't want *that!*"

"We want to go that way," Trina pointed. "See the sign with the green dot?"

Erin looked dismayed. "We're going on a green slope? That's so easy! All the little kids use that."

"I promised my parents we'd take that one first," Katie said. "So the instructor can evaluate us. Then we can move on to a blue slope." She glanced uneasily at Sarah. She was the only one among them who hadn't skied before, and she didn't pick up on sports very quickly. How would she feel if they all left her behind? But it was either that or being stuck on a baby slope all week.

"Do we have to go on one of those things that carry you up the mountain?" Sarah asked nervously. "They look scary to me."

"Not for the beginner slope," Trina assured her. "They have a rope tow. You just hold onto it, and it drags you up the hill. See?" They'd reached the rope, and took their places in line. Others got in line behind them.

"Now hold on tight," Katie instructed Sarah.

The rope began to move. And Megan, the last of the five girls in line, immediately lost her balance. Jerked backwards, she toppled, and knocked down the people behind her.

"Megan!" Erin moaned.

"Well, I'm not used to the rope," Megan grumbled as she struggled to her feet.

It was a small hill, so it didn't take long to reach the top. An instructor met them up there, and formed them into a group. Just as Erin had feared, the others in their group were little kids, all giggling like hyenas.

Katie barely listened or watched as the instructor started telling them how to stand. He demonstrated the positions for turning and stopping. It was all basic stuff, and except for Sarah, the girls had all heard it before.

Finally, the instructor led them off. It was a pleasant run down the hill, but for Katie, it was over much too quickly. Seconds later, she was forming a snowplow at the bottom. So did the others.

Except for poor Sarah. She took a fall—and slid down the hill on her rear end.

She managed to get herself to where the others were gathered around the instructor. He lifted his goggles to the top of his head. "You all can go on to a blue slope," the instructor told Katie, Erin, Megan, and Trina.

He smiled kindly at Sarah. "But I think you'd better stay here for a while and have a few more lessons."

Sarah didn't look at all disappointed. Relief spread across her face.

"I'll stay here with you," Megan offered.

"You don't have to," Sarah objected.

"I want to," Megan insisted. "Really. It's been ages since I've skied, and I could use some instruction. Like a refresher course."

Katie knew Megan was only offering this so Sarah wouldn't have to ski alone. At Sunnyside, Megan and Sarah were best friends, and there were lots of times when Megan tailored her activities so Sarah could follow along. Katie would have done the same for Trina. But thank goodness, she didn't have to.

Katie, Erin, and Trina moved to the trail leading to an intermediate hill. "Is this where your brothers ski?" Erin asked casually.

"Sometimes," Katie said. "They claim they're going straight to the expert slopes, but I bet my parents will make them do a couple of practice runs on an intermediate slope. They haven't done all that much skiing."

They joined the line waiting for lifts up the

hill. "Now, this is going to be real skiing," Katie said excitedly to Trina. "Have you ever been on one of these hills before?"

Trina nodded. "With my father. Taking the lift is almost as much fun as skiing down the hill!"

She was right. Sitting in the lift, climbing up in the air, Katie felt like she was on an amusement park ride. When they arrived at the top and got off, her heart began to pound. This was so much higher than the easy slope!

But she knew she could handle it. With her knees bent and her back arched, she pushed off.

It was glorious! The run down the hill seemed to go on and on. Katie had to concentrate a lot more than she'd had to do on the easy slope. It wasn't too steep, so she didn't pick up much speed, but that was fine—she managed to sail along at a steady and even pace. When she saw Trina move past her, she used her poles to give herself a push. Still, Trina was at the bottom before she was.

"You beat me," Katie said. "But you've had more practice than I have."

Trina pushed back her goggles and laughed. "I didn't know we were having a race."

Katie grinned. "Okay, you've been warned! Hey, where's Erin?"

"Here she comes." The figure in hot pink moved slowly but gracefully toward them, ending in a neat christie.

"Want to race now?" Katie asked her eagerly.

"Oh, Katie, honestly." Erin looked around. "This is a good slope. There are lots of cute guys skiing it."

"How can you tell?" Katie asked. "They've all got their faces covered."

Trina giggled. "Erin's got radar. She doesn't have to be able to see them. She can tell when there's a cute guy within a mile of her."

They headed back to the lift. On the next trip down the hill, Katie reached the bottom before Trina, but she suspected Trina had slowed down intentionally. It didn't matter, though. She was having too much fun to care about competition.

After their third time, Erin announced that she was going back to the lodge. "I want to get ready for lunch."

"It's not lunchtime yet," Katie objected.

"I want to change and fix my hair," Erin

said. "Um, will your brothers be eating with us?"

"Not if I can help it," Katie replied.

To her surprise, Erin didn't seem dismayed. "That's okay. Actually, I'd just as soon be free to check out other possibilities." She skied off.

Katie and Trina went back up the hill. Katie figured they had time for two more trips down. But after the first, her stomach was growling. "I'm getting hungry," she told Trina.

"Me too. Let's head back."

They were nearing the lodge, when Trina announced, "Here come your brothers."

"Ignore them," Katie directed her.

But Trina was too polite for that. "Hi, Peter, Michael. Did you have a good morning?"

Carrying their skis over their shoulders, the boys grinned at them. "Sure did," Michael said. "Did you girls have fun on the bunny slopes?"

Katie grinned right back. "For your information, we've been skiing an intermediate slope."

"Where have you guys been?" Trina asked.

"On the black diamond slopes."

Katie gritted her teeth.

"In fact," Peter said casually, "we just came down the Monster."

"What's the Monster?" Katie asked, but she had a sinking suspicion she knew. The name was a dead giveaway.

If it was possible, their cocky grins got even cockier. "Only the toughest slope here," Michael said.

"It's for *serious* skiers," Peter added. The unspoken words "not like you" hung in the air.

The boys ambled away. "Show-offs," Katie murmured.

Trina turned to her. "There's a big difference between intermediate slopes and expert slopes. That Monster one sounds dangerous. I hope they're good enough to handle it."

"They *think* they're wonderful," Katie said through clenched teeth. "The slope couldn't be all that tough if they're able to ski it."

"It must be hard," Trina insisted, "if it's got a name like the Monster. Maybe your brothers are better at skiing than you think they are."

Katie would never in a million years admit that what Trina said was true. "Huh. I'll bet you and I could ski the Monster."

Trina shivered. "No, thanks. I haven't had that much practice. And don't you think about it either, Katie Dillon. This is our first day. I don't think we're ready for a really expert slope."

If anyone else in the world had said something like that to her, Katie would have been offended.

But Trina was her best friend. And more than that. With reluctance, Katie had to admit that what Trina said was probably true.

Chapter 4

"What a great day!" Katie's eyes were bright and her cheeks were flushed as she plopped down on the sofa in their suite. "Those intermediate slopes were a lot easier than I thought they would be."

Trina laughed. "Katie, you're bragging. I saw you take a couple of falls out there."

"Everyone falls once in a while," Katie said. "Even professional skiers."

"You didn't hurt yourself when you fell, did you?" Sarah asked anxiously.

"Nah," Katie replied. "The snow's so soft, it cushions the fall."

"It's funny about that snow," Sarah mused. "How come there's so much soft snow up here? I saw hardly any snow on the way here."

"It's not real snow," Megan informed her.

"It's made by machines, especially for skiing." She turned to the others. "You guys should have seen Sarah. She's really improved, considering she's never skied before."

"Do you think you'll be ready for the intermediate slopes tomorrow?" Trina asked Sarah.

Sarah shook her head. "No, I don't want to rush into anything. I better spend another day where I was today. But Megan, you don't have to stay on the baby slope with me tomorrow. I know it must be pretty boring for you."

Katie spoke casually. "I think I might be ready to move on from the intermediate slopes."

Trina put her hands on her hips and gazed at Katie sternly. "After one day? No way, Katie. Those expert slopes can be brutal. All those moguls and stuff."

"How do you know?" Katie challenged her. "You ever been on one?"

"No, but—"

"Erin, have you?" Katie asked.

Erin was pulling stuff out of her suitcase. "Have I what?"

"Have you ever been on an advanced slope?"

"No . . . darn, where are those shoes?"

"What are you doing?" Sarah asked.

"Trying to figure out what I'm going to change into," Erin said.

"Getting all dressed up just for us?" Megan teased.

"No, silly," Erin murmured. "I'm just going to put on some après-ski wear."

Megan's eyes widened. "Some *what* wear?"

"Après-ski," Trina echoed. " 'Après' is French for 'after.' She must mean what you wear after you ski."

"Exactly," Erin said. She pulled her makeup bag from the suitcase.

"Why do you need something special to wear after skiing?" Megan asked in bewilderment.

"Because that's the best time at a ski resort," Erin said. She could tell from their blank expressions that they didn't know what she was talking about, but she didn't want to waste time explaining. They'd figure it out.

She gathered her stuff and went into one of

the bathrooms. Alone behind the closed door, she dropped her attitude of nonchalance and shivered in excitement. At lunch in the lodge, sitting with the girls, she'd taken the opportunity to scope out the other guests at the resort.

There were so many cute guys! In particular, she noticed a group of teenagers, very cool, who made Katie's brothers look like little kids.

Brushing her hair, she recalled the looks on her friends' faces when she told them she was going to a ski resort for the vacation instead of a health spa. They'd all been skiing before, so they weren't anywhere near as impressed. But if she could go back with tales of a great romantic encounter—wow! They'd be green with envy.

Of course, she could always invent a story for them. But since she'd never had a holiday romance before, she wasn't sure if she could make it convincing. It would be much better to have the real experience to tell.

She finished applying her makeup and examined herself critically. Yes, she could definitely pass for fourteen.

She pulled on beige leggings, and topped them with a long sweater of soft blue and beige wool. It was perfect—casual but sophisticated.

Back in the living room, Erin saw that the others had changed into jeans and sweatshirts. They were lying around, watching some dumb TV show. They all looked pretty beat after the first day of skiing. Erin frowned. It wasn't going to be easy to make them move. But she didn't want to go over to the lodge by herself.

"Come on, you guys, let's go over to the lodge and check it out."

"It's not time for dinner yet," Katie objected.

"But people hang out there," Erin said.

Sarah yawned and snuggled up on the sofa. "I'm happy just to hang out here."

Erin gritted her teeth in frustration. Luckily, Megan came to her rescue. "I wouldn't mind seeing the lodge. Hey, maybe we can get a deck of cards there. I learned this neat card game I could teach you guys."

"Sounds good to me," Trina said. "We can hang around this room anytime."

Sarah pulled herself off the sofa. "Yeah, if I stay here I'll fall asleep."

On their way out, Megan said, "There's one problem with this card game. Only four can play."

"That's okay," Erin said. "I'll just watch. I'm not very good at cards anyway."

The scene in the lodge lived up to Erin's expectations. Even though it was a big room, the beamed ceiling and blazing fire made it seem cozy. There were lots of people gathered in small clusters, and the atmosphere was like a very relaxed party.

While Megan went off in search of playing cards, the others found a table. Trina, Sarah, and Katie sat down, but Erin remained standing and scanned the room. She spotted the group of teenagers she'd seen at lunch, gathered around the fire.

Megan returned. "I got the cards." She sat down at the table and began dealing them. "Okay, it's a complicated game, so pay attention. Everyone gets eight cards to start."

Erin tuned her out and focused on the group of teenagers. There was one boy in particular she had her eyes on. He was slender and fair haired. She watched as he moved away from the group and began looking at some framed photos on a wall. Near the display, there was a bar where people were getting steaming cups of something.

"I think they're selling cocoa over there," Erin said. "You guys want some?"

There was a general bobbing of heads from the cardplayers. Erin ambled toward the bar. As she passed the boy, she paused as if a photo caught her eye. Recognizing the picture, she inadvertently uttered an "oh!"

The boy turned. "What did you say?"

Erin pointed at the photo. "Isn't that Rod Laney?"

The boy looked. "Yeah, I think so." He moved in closer and peered at the scrawled autograph.

"I wonder why his picture is here."

The boy gestured at the whole display. "I think these are all famous people who have stayed here. Looks pretty goofy, huh?"

Erin smiled. "He's actually nice, though. Rod Laney."

The boy's eyebrows went up. "You know him?"

"I met him once. Actually, we worked on a film."

Now he looked really impressed. "Are you an actress?"

Erin laughed lightly. "Not exactly. He was in a film that was being shot at my summer camp last summer." She didn't add that her only connection with the film was as a stand-in for an actress—and that she'd been fired from the job after a day.

"You were at a summer camp?"

On no, Erin groaned silently. She'd blown it. Now he'd know she was younger. Frantically, she tried to think of a way out of it. But he provided the way.

"Were you a counselor or something?"

Erin smiled. "Mmm . . . I'm Erin Chapman."

He extended his right hand. "Josh Patterson."

What super manners older guys have, Erin thought as they shook hands. "Where are you from?" she asked.

"New York. I'm here with a club from my high school."

The last words sent a thrill through her.

High school. He had to be at least fifteen. Maybe sixteen!

"Would you like to get some hot chocolate?" he asked.

Erin smiled brightly. "Love some!"

Katie grimaced as she examined her hand. Crummy cards, she thought. Oh, how she hated to lose games. "Where's our cocoa? I thought Erin was getting some for us."

Trina glanced toward the other side of the room and smiled. "I think Erin's got something else on her mind."

Katie turned to look. There was Erin, sitting at a little table with a boy. Katie scowled.

"I should have known," she grumbled. She watched as Erin laughed, tossed her head so her blonde hair cascaded around her shoulders, and gave the boy a sidelong look. She'd seen her do that move at the socials Camp Sunnyside had with Camp Eagle.

"Disgusting," Katie commented. "You'd think that's what she came here for. Honestly, I'll bet Erin's more interested in flirting than skiing."

Sarah chuckled. "Of course she is! Erin's more interested in flirting than anything."

Katie sniffed. "Disgusting," she said again.

Trina just smiled. "That's our Erin," she said mildly. "Oh, Katie, here come your parents."

Katie turned her head and waved. Her parents strolled over to them. "Having a good time, girls?" Mr. Dillon asked.

"Fantastic," Trina said. "We went on the intermediate slopes today!"

"That's great," Mrs. Dillon said.

"But be careful," Mr. Dillon cautioned. "Some of those slopes can be trickier than they look."

"Did you know that Peter and Michael went on an expert slope?" Katie asked. She crossed her fingers, hoping they didn't.

To her disappointment, they nodded. "The instructor felt they were ready for it," Mrs. Dillon said. She looked around. "Where's Erin?"

Katie scowled. "Over there." Her parents glanced at the table where Erin was sitting with the boy. Katie expected to see looks of disapproval on their faces. Instead, she saw amused smiles. "Well, we're going to get some dinner. Would you like to join us?"

The girls decided it would be more fun to eat by themselves later, and Katie's parents left. Only moments later, two other members of the Dillon family approached the table. "What are you guys playing?" Peter asked.

"It's a new card game," Megan told them. "Hey, did you guys really go on the Monster?"

"Yep," Michael said. "It's no big deal, really."

"Hah!" Peter shook his head. "Don't let him pull your leg. The Monster's brutal." He wagged a finger at the girls and affected a stern look. "Don't let me catch any of you kids near there."

As they wandered off, Katie automatically stuck her tongue out at their backs. Sarah, however, was gazing after them in awe. "They must be really good, Katie. I heard people talking about the Monster today."

Katie rolled her eyes. "It can't be that brutal if Peter and Michael can handle it."

Trina looked at her suspiciously. "Katie, I hope you're not getting any crazy ideas."

Katie just shrugged. She was getting lots of

ideas. As for whether or not they were crazy—well, that was a matter of opinion.

The next day, on the slopes, Katie kept seeing her brothers' faces in her head. That obnoxious look of superiority they wore the night before as they bragged about skiing the Monster—she couldn't stop thinking about it.

She wasn't concentrating the way she should, and she hit a bump. A split second later, she was sitting in the snow, feeling a little dazed.

Megan drew up beside her. "You okay?"

Katie got up and brushed off the snow. "Sure." She looked around. "I was daydreaming. You know, I think this hill's a little boring."

"Boring!" Megan gazed at her strangely. "Are you nuts? It's fantastic!"

Katie cocked her head. "Don't you think it would be neat to try something tougher?"

"Like what?"

"Like a black diamond slope."

Megan looked uncertain. "I wouldn't want to try it without having an instructor evaluate us. Maybe you're ready, but I don't think the rest of us are."

"Oh, come on," Katie urged. "If Peter and Michael can handle it, we can."

Megan gasped. "Are you talking about the Monster? Forget it, Katie!"

Katie sighed. Together, the two girls pushed off and continued down the hill. Ahead of them, they could see Trina, her graceful form seeming to move effortlessly over the snow. Katie admired the way she handled herself.

They met at the bottom. "Trina, you're really good," Katie said.

"Thanks," Trina said. "I feel like I'm making real improvement."

"Personally, I think you could take on the Monster," Katie said, trying to sound very casual.

But Trina knew Katie too well. "You're not going to con me into going on that hill, Katie Dillon."

"Let's go," Megan said. "We've got time for one more trip down the hill before lunch."

"Where's Erin?" Katie asked. "Oh, I see her coming. You guys go on. We'll catch up."

She watched as Erin came down the hill. She wasn't a bad skier, Katie thought. She didn't move as fast as Trina, but her form was good.

Oh, how she wanted to go down that Monster. She could just see herself, casually running into the twins at the top of the hill. She could picture the stunned expressions on their faces as she calmly proceeded to push off. Her brothers thought they were so hot. If Katie could make it down the Monster without a spill, that would really put them in their place.

But she didn't want to try it alone. If only she could talk Trina or Megan into going down the Monster with her! Remembering their reactions just now, she was resigned to the fact that she'd never talk them into it.

She waved to catch Erin's attention. Then, in the back of her head, a tiny spark of an idea appeared. And began to grow.

Did she dare? Okay, maybe it wasn't a nice thing to do. But it was only a tiny little lie. It wouldn't hurt anyone.

Erin snowplowed just a few feet away. Before she could lose her nerve, Katie shuffled over to her. "Erin, I just saw that guy you were talking to in the lodge yesterday."

Erin pushed back her goggles, and her eyes lit up. "Josh? Where is he?"

Katie swallowed. "Uh, he said he was going down the Monster. I think he said something about wanting to meet you there."

The eagerness in Erin's eyes made her feel guilty. "He did? What's the Monster?"

"Oh, one of the black diamond slopes," Katie said. "It's supposed to be tougher, but my brothers have been skiing it so it can't be all that bad."

Erin considered this. "I wouldn't want to go up there by myself. I mean, I wouldn't want him to think I'm that anxious to see him."

"I'll go with you," Katie offered.

"Yeah? Okay, let's go."

They found the trail leading to the Monster, and waited in line for the lift. Katie couldn't help but notice that they were the youngest people preparing to go down the Monster. She hoped Erin didn't notice.

But Erin was happily chattering away about Josh. "He's in high school! And he's so sophisticated and mature. I'll bet he's got a girlfriend back home. But maybe not. Ooh, maybe we could have a long distance romance."

Katie barely listened. She was noticing how steep this hill was. A combination of excitement and fear churned in her stomach.

When they got off the lift, Erin whispered, "Don't be real obvious. Just look around and see if he's here."

"It's hard to tell, with everyone wearing goggles and hats and scarves," Katie said.

"You're right. I guess I'll just have to let him find me."

"Maybe he's waiting at the bottom," Katie suggested.

As they moved toward the edge of the hill, Erin stopped suddenly. "Uh, Katie, this is a *lot* bigger than the hills we've been skiing. And it's really steep."

"It just looks that way from here," Katie assured her. "Once we push off, you won't be able to tell the difference."

Erin looked doubtful. But she followed Katie, and together they started down the hill.

It *was* steep, even steeper than it seemed. Katie could feel herself picking up speed. Too much speed. She tried to use her edges to control herself by turning sideways into the hill.

Erin flew past her. Her arms were stretched

out, as though she'd frozen into a position. She's not in control at all, Katie thought worriedly.

Then Erin lost a pole. An arm reached out wildly for it. She completely lost her balance. One of her skis flew out from under her. In horror, Katie watched as Erin flew into the air—and landed back on the snow in a crumpled heap.

Chapter 5

Katie was still shaking as she huddled on the sofa in the chalet. Trina, Sarah, and Megan were gathered around her, their eyes wide as they listened to her story.

"It was awful!" Katie's voice trembled. "She was just lying there, not moving at all. I thought she was dead."

"What did you do?" Sarah asked.

"I tried to get over to her, but I kept sliding in the snow. Finally I got there, and she was moaning so at least I knew she was alive. Then the ski patrol came down the hill on this huge sled, and they tied her to it and took her down." Katie paused to catch her breath.

"Where did they take her?" Megan asked impatiently.

"They told me they were taking her to the first aid station." Katie could barely get the next words out, they frightened her so much. "But she looked like she needed more than first aid to me."

Trina placed a comforting hand on Katie's arm. "She might not be hurt badly. I've seen people taken away on that sled when they had nothing worse than a twisted ankle."

Katie swallowed. "I guess. I told my parents and they went to the first aid station. They're supposed to call here as soon as they find out what's wrong with her." She looked at the telephone, willing it to ring.

The others were silent. Katie knew they were all sharing the same fear. But she couldn't keep it to herself. "Oh, what if she's really hurt bad? I feel so awful!"

"We all feel bad about this," Trina told her.

"But I feel worse," Katie moaned. She twisted her hands together. "I think I must be a terrible person."

Megan gazed at her blankly. Then her expression cleared. "Oh, I get it. You feel bad because you were saying mean things about Erin last night."

"It's more than that," Katie murmured.

Trina's eyes narrowed. "Katie, where did this accident happen?"

Katie bit her lip. "I told you. While we were skiing."

"While you were skiing *where?*"

Katie took a deep breath. They were going to find out sooner or later. "On the Monster," she whispered.

There was a gasp. "What were you doing on the Monster!" Sarah asked in bewilderment.

"Katie!" Trina exclaimed. "You talked Erin into going down the Monster?"

Katie nodded, her face flushed with shame.

"But how?" Megan demanded. "Erin's not that great a skier, and she knows it."

"I lied to her," Katie admitted. "I told her that boy she was with last night wanted to meet her there."

Her confession was met with a dead silence. Katie forced herself to look at her friends. She'd never seen Trina look so angry. Megan and Sarah were aghast.

Katie couldn't bear it. She knew she deserved everything they were feeling about her. "I know. It's my fault, it's all my fault." And then she did something she hardly ever did. She started to cry. "If anything's really wrong with Erin, I'll never forgive myself," she sobbed.

Even through her tears, she could see Trina's expression soften. "Katie, there's nothing you can do about it now. What you did was wrong, and you know that, but—"

Before she could finish, the phone rang. Megan grabbed it. "Hello?" Then she held it out toward Katie. "It's your mother."

Hastily, Katie wiped her eyes on her sleeve and went to the phone. "Mom? How's Erin?"

"She's going to be all right, Katie. It's just a sprained ankle. We'll be back in a few minutes."

Katie was practically faint with relief. Hanging up, she reported her mother's news to the others.

"Thank goodness!" Megan exclaimed.

"Will she be going home?" Sarah asked.

"I don't know," Katie said. "They're bringing her back here for now." She shivered, and realized she'd been sitting around in her wet ski clothes. "I'm going to change," she told the others. She went into the bedroom. Trina followed.

"Erin was lucky," Katie said.

"So were you," Trina replied. "Katie, if

she'd been seriously injured, you would have been responsible."

"I know," Katie said. "I just hope Erin doesn't find that out."

"She will," Trina stated.

"How?"

"You're going to tell her."

Katie stared at Trina in disbelief. "Why would I do that?"

"Because if you don't, your conscience is going to bother you for a long time. Maybe forever."

Trina was right. Still, Katie's stomach turned over at the thought of confessing to Erin. "She'll be furious with me!"

Trina nodded. "Probably. But she'll get over it, when she sees how truly sorry you are."

Slowly, Katie nodded. "I hope so." She put on some jeans and a sweater, and the girls went back into the living room. Megan was peering out the window.

"Here she comes."

The girls gathered around to watch. Katie's mother was helping Erin out of the car. Erin leaned against her while Mr. Dillon pulled something from the backseat.

"It's a wheelchair!" Sarah exclaimed. "Poor Erin!"

When the shock of seeing Erin in a wheelchair wore off, Katie noticed something almost equally shocking. "Look at her hair," she said softly.

The others would know what she meant. For Erin to be out in public with her hair a mess, she had to be feeling pretty sick.

The girls ran to the door and held it open. Erin looked pale and dazed, and her ankle was wrapped in an elastic bandage.

"Here we are," Mrs. Dillon said brightly.

Katie reached down and clutched Erin's hand. "Oh, Erin, we were so worried about you."

Erin's gaze wavered, as if she wasn't quite sure she recognized Katie. "Huh?"

"The doctor gave her something for the pain, so she's a little sleepy," Mr. Dillon explained.

"Do her parents know what happened?" Trina asked.

"We haven't been able to reach them in Texas," Mrs. Dillon said. "We left a message at their hotel. Erin, why don't we help you get onto the sofa?"

The adults pulled her gently from the chair and lowered her onto the sofa.

"Can we get you anything?" Mr. Dillon asked.

Erin shook her head. "No, thank you."

"We'll get her anything she wants," Katie said quickly. She wanted her parents to leave. Telling Erin what she had done was going to be hard enough, without having her parents hear also.

Finally, her parents left, and the girls clustered around Erin.

"Does it hurt very much?" Sarah asked.

"It aches a little," Erin said. She gazed at her ankle glumly. "I can't believe this. My holiday is ruined. My parents will probably come to take me home, and I'll spend my whole vacation sitting in my room alone."

If Katie had felt guilty before, it was nothing compared to how rotten she felt now. "Maybe they'll let you stay here."

"What's the point?" Erin sighed. "It's not like I can do any more skiing."

"At least here, you'll have us to keep you company," Megan pointed out.

Erin managed a small smile. "Thanks, Megan. But I wouldn't want to keep you guys off the slopes." She shook her head. "It's my own fault, for chasing after that boy. I should never have gone up on that Monster. And I didn't even see Josh."

Katie felt three pairs of eyes on her. It was confession time. "Erin . . . Josh wasn't there."

Erin forehead furrowed. "Huh?"

"I never saw Josh. I made that story up to get you to go on the Monster with me."

She'd never before seen Erin speechless. Maybe whatever the doctor gave her for the pain had muddled her brain. Maybe she didn't really understand what Katie had said.

But then Erin's eyes darkened. Her lips parted. And Katie knew she'd gotten through.

"You—you tricked me? It's your fault that this happened to me?"

Katie wished hopelessly for a hole to open up in the floor so she could drop into it. Mutely, she nodded.

"How could you do that to me?"

Katie shook her head in misery. "I'm sorry, Erin. I'm truly, truly sorry."

"Well, your being sorry doesn't do me much good, does it? It doesn't fix anything!" Then Erin yawned, and her eyelids drooped. "Katie Dillon . . . I'm never going to . . ." She yawned again. "Never . . . forgive you. . . ." The last words trailed off. Erin was asleep.

Trina put her arm around Katie. "She's angry and upset right now. She's not going to hate you forever."

Katie couldn't take her eyes off the sleeping figure. Was Trina right? Could Erin ever forgive her?

And even if Erin did . . . could Katie ever forgive herself? Katie blinked back tears. "I wouldn't blame Erin if she hated me forever. What I did was terrible. But I'm going to make it up to her."

"How?" Sarah asked.

"I don't know yet." Katie faced them all solemnly. "But I'll think of a way."

Half awake, Erin shifted her position on the sofa. A twinge in her ankle forced her eyes open. For a minute, she wasn't exactly sure where she was. Then she realized she was sleeping on the sofa, in the chalet, at the ski resort.

But then she noticed the sunlight streaming in from the window. She saw the clock that read three o'clock. What was she doing, sleeping in the middle of the afternoon?

Then it all came back to her. The fall on the hill. The first aid station.

She swung her legs off the sofa and touched the floor gingerly. Slowly, she got up, and applied a little pressure to the foot with the injured ankle. It wasn't too bad. She tried walking. She had to limp, in order to favor the bad ankle, but the pain wasn't terrible.

Still, she wouldn't be able to ski. Her vacation was ruined. And all because of Katie.

She heard movements behind the closed door to one of the bedrooms, and she moved quickly back to the sofa. Maybe she wasn't seriously injured, but she didn't want Katie to know that. The worse off Katie thought Erin was, the worse Katie would feel. And Erin wanted Katie to feel as bad as possible.

Trina came out of a bedroom. "Erin! You're awake! How are you feeling?"

Erin hoisted herself up on her elbows. "Okay, I guess. Where is everyone?"

"We thought you might be hungry when you woke up, so I sent them off to the lodge to get some sandwiches." Trina went to the window. "Here they come now."

The girls burst in. "Erin! How are you?" Megan asked.

Erin offered a very weak, brave smile. "I'll be all right. I think."

"We brought you sandwiches," Katie said eagerly. "Are you hungry?"

Erin closed her eyes a minute. "I . . . I don't have any appetite at all."

"You should try to eat something," Trina insisted.

Erin smiled bravely. "Yes, you're right. I'll try."

Katie dug into her bag. "I brought roast beef, tuna, and ham and cheese. Which do you want?"

"Oh. No chicken?"

Katie checked again. "No. Just roast beef, tuna, ham and cheese. But if you want a chicken sandwich, I'll go back and get you one."

"Oh, that would be nice, Katie."

She watched with approval as Katie raced out the door.

"Does your ankle hurt?" Megan asked.

Erin closed her eyes tightly and clenched her fists, as if she was in terrible pain. Then she opened her eyes. "No, not very much." From the look of sympathy in Megan's eyes,

Erin knew it had been a convincing performance.

Actually, she was amazed to find she didn't feel particularly bad at all. But she didn't want the others to know she wasn't suffering. Especially Katie.

The object of her anger returned with a chicken sandwich. "Thank you," Erin said. "You know, you guys don't have to hang around here with me all day. You can go over to the lodge. I don't really mind being left alone."

"We wouldn't leave you by yourself," Megan argued.

"Actually, you could come to the lodge, Erin," Sarah said. "It's flat all the way, and we could wheel you."

It was on the tip of Erin's tongue to say "But I can walk," when it occurred to her that being in a wheelchair would make her look much more injured than she was. Besides, limping wouldn't get her nearly as much attention.

"But I look so awful," she murmured.

"We'll fix you up," Trina said cheerfully.

Over the next half hour, they all got an opportunity to help Erin. Trina washed Erin's hair in the sink and blew it dry. Megan held a mirror in front of Erin's face so she could put on her makeup. Sarah painted her fingernails.

"I think it's going to be too painful to pull pants on over my ankle," Erin noted. "I've got a skirt, but I'm sure it's wrinkled."

"I'll iron it for you," Katie offered.

"Why, thank you," Erin replied.

Katie wasn't very good at ironing. Every time she held it up for Erin's approval, Erin pointed out a wrinkle she'd missed.

Finally, they were ready to go to the lodge. Katie pushed the wheelchair, while the others hovered on both sides. When they entered the lodge, the first person Erin saw was Josh. He hurried over.

"What happened to you?" he asked.

Erin was delighted by the concern on his face. "I took a fall. I'm not that expert a skier, and I guess I was on a slope that I shouldn't have been on."

"Which slope?"

"The Monster."

"The Monster!" Josh's eyebrows went up. "I've run that. It's famous for being pretty tough. Why did you try it?"

Erin gave Katie a sidelong look. Katie was staring at the ground.

"Silly of me, wasn't it?" Erin said lightly.

"How long will you be in the wheelchair?" Josh asked.

Erin considered her answer. A few other people had gathered around, and the Sunnyside girls were still there too. This was her chance to play up her accident. She wasn't about to tell them she'd only been given the wheelchair at the first aid station because she was too drowsy to walk.

"The doctor didn't know," she said softly. "I could be in this chair for . . . a long time."

Murmurs of sympathy and concern swept over the group. Other skiers stopped by to ask how she was. Everyone was terribly nice. She couldn't remember ever having this much attention in her life!

She told the story about her fall on the Monster over and over. Each person who heard it oohed and ahhed and seemed impressed that she'd lived through the experience. People kept offering to get her hot chocolate or a soda or anything she wanted. Her wheelchair began to feel like a throne!

But she wasn't able to enjoy it for long. It

had been a wild day, and she began to feel tired. "I'll push you back," Josh offered.

"Thanks, Josh, but Katie will help me," Erin said. "Katie!"

Katie scurried to her side. "Yes? Can I get you something?"

"I think I'd like to go back to the chalet now," Erin said.

Trina joined them, but Katie insisted on doing the pushing. Erin could tell by the way Katie was breathing heavily that the chair wasn't easy to push.

Just as they entered the chalet, Erin uttered a soft, "Oh, no."

"What's the matter?" Trina asked.

"I wanted to bring back a cup of hot chocolate," Erin said. "Katie, do you think—"

"Sure," Katie said. "No problem. I'll get it."

The phone rang, and Trina picked it up. "Hello! Oh yes, just a minute please. Erin, it's your mother." She wheeled Erin to the phone.

"Darling, what's wrong?" her mother asked. "We've got a message here from Mrs. Dillon."

"I took a fall on the slopes, Mom. And I sprained my ankle."

"Oh, no! Are you all right?"

Erin watched as Trina disappeared into a bathroom. She lowered her voice. "I'm absolutely fine, Mom, no big deal."

"I'll fly up there first thing in the morning to take you home," Mrs. Chapman said.

"No, Mom, don't do that," Erin said quickly. "I'm fine here!"

It took a while to convince her mother that she should stay at the resort. But in the end, as usual, Erin got her way.

She was hanging up the phone just as Katie returned with her hot chocolate. "I hope it's still warm," Katie said.

Erin took a sip, and wrinkled her nose. "Well, it's not *cold.*"

"Did you talk to your parents?" Katie asked.

Erin nodded. "They wanted to come get me, but I said I'd rather stay here."

"Good." Katie hesitated. "Erin, I really am so sorry. I know you're angry at me, and I don't blame you. But I'll do anything I can to make it up to you."

Erin didn't reply. She took another sip of the hot chocolate, and gazed at Katie over the rim.

She could tell Katie really did feel pretty

awful about all this. Why, she was practically offering to become Erin's slave!

And then she recalled the scene at the lodge, where she had reigned as princess in her wheelchair. Okay, she might not be able to do any more skiing.

But there were other ways to have a good time.

Chapter 6

"Are you sure you don't want us to stay here with you?" Trina asked anxiously. Dressed in skiing clothes, she stood with Megan and Sarah at the door of the chalet the next morning.

Erin, in her wheelchair, gave them all a sad-but-brave little smile. "No, you guys go on. Have fun. Katie will keep me company."

"I'll take care of her," Katie assured them.

Sarah spoke with admiration. "Gee, Erin, you're being such a good sport about this."

"Yeah," Megan agreed. "Some people would be whining and complaining and feeling sorry for themselves."

Erin lowered her head in modesty. "There's no point in that. I have to make the best of this. You can't cry over spilled milk and all that."

The girls still seemed reluctant to leave. "Go on," Erin urged. "I'll be just fine."

"We'll see you at lunch," Trina said, and they left.

"What would you like to do?" Katie asked Erin. "I've got a travel Scrabble game."

Erin shook her head. "I think I'm too weak for that, Katie. Could you get me a pillow? My back is so stiff."

Katie disappeared into a bedroom, and returned a second later with a pillow. Erin leaned forward while Katie put it in the chair. Then Erin frowned.

"This one's too soft. Could you see if there's a firmer one?"

"I think they're all the same," Katie said.

Erin raised her eyebrows. "Well, you could check, couldn't you?"

"Oh, sure," Katie said hastily. She hurried back into the bedroom. At that moment, there was a knock on the door.

"Katie!" Erin called. "Could you get the door?" She knew she was perfectly able to get it herself. But why should she bother when she had Katie at her beck and call?

Katie hurried back out from the bedroom

and went to the door. "Hi, Mom, Dad. Come on in."

"We wanted to see how Erin's coming along," her father said. "Ah, there she is." He sat down on the sofa, and Katie's mother sat down next to him.

"How are you feeling, dear?" Mrs. Dillon asked.

Erin smiled sweetly. "Much better, thank you. A little weak, of course."

"In all the excitement yesterday, I never found out how you came to fall like that," Mr. Dillon said. "What happened?"

Erin glanced at Katie, who was standing behind the sofa. Her face was pale, and her eyes made a silent plea to Erin. Erin glanced down at the injury that was keeping her off the slopes. What a chance to get even this was. If Katie's parents knew how Erin got that injury, Katie would be in serious trouble.

And then, she had a flash of memory. Camp Sunnyside. All the fun, the good times, the happiness in cabin six. And especially the time Katie came to her rescue when some older girls almost got Erin into real trouble.

She turned to the Dillons. "I guess I just

didn't look where I was going. I must have hit an icy patch on the hill."

She didn't miss the wave of relief that crossed Katie's face. She wished she could send a message with her eyes, something like, Don't think you're completely off the hook, Katie Dillon. It didn't matter, though. Katie would figure that out.

"Let us know if you need anything," Mrs. Dillon said.

"Thank you," Erin replied. As soon as they left, Katie rushed over to her.

"Erin, thanks a lot for not telling my parents. I think I would have been grounded till I was sixty-five."

Erin waved a hand. "Forget it. Katie, I'm a little cold. Would you bring me a sweater? My suitcases are in that bedroom."

Katie went into the bedroom. She returned a moment later with a green pullover. "Here you are."

Erin made a face. "Not that one. I feel like wearing the light blue one."

Katie took the green sweater back into the bedroom. A few minutes later, she called out, "Erin, I can't find a light blue one."

"Keep looking," Erin called back. "It's in

there somewhere." She smiled to herself. She knew exactly where her light blue sweater was. Neatly folded and tucked away in a drawer back home.

Moments later, red faced, Katie emerged from the bedroom. "Erin, honestly, I've practically emptied those suitcases. And there's no blue sweater."

"Oh. Maybe I didn't bring it. Well, why don't you bring out all my sweaters and I'll decide which one I feel like wearing right now."

Katie looked at her quizzically. "What does it matter which sweater you wear? No one's going to see you here but us."

Erin didn't reply. She just gazed at Katie evenly. Katie shrugged, and went back into the bedroom. When she returned, she was carrying six sweaters. She laid them out on the sofa for Erin to examine.

Erin studied them for a moment. Then she said, "You know, now I'm feeling warm. I don't want to wear a sweater after all."

She could have sworn she saw Katie's lips tighten for a second.

"I think I'd like to watch television," she said. "Would you turn it on for me?"

Katie obliged.

"I can't see it from here."

Katie got behind the wheelchair and moved it in front of the television.

"That's too close," Erin said.

Katie pulled it back.

"That's too far."

"How's this?" Katie asked, pushing it slightly closer.

"That's good. Ick, I hate game shows. See if you can find a soap opera."

Katie switched the channel. "Here's one."

Erin grimaced. "I don't like that one. Can you find another one?"

"Here's a remote control box," Katie said. She handed it to Erin.

"Thanks." Then Erin squinted. "The sun's in my eyes, Katie. Maybe you could close the blinds."

Katie went to the windows and twisted the rod.

"Now it's too dark. Switch on the light, would you? No, not that one, the other one." As soon as Katie did that, Erin went on. "I can hardly hear the TV. Would you turn it up, please?"

"You've got the remote," Katie said. "You can adjust the volume."

"I can't figure out which button to press."

Katie took the remote from her and turned up the sound. Then she sat down on the sofa.

"This show is boring," Erin commented. "Katie, get me my magazine, the one I brought from home."

"Where is it?" Katie asked.

"Somewhere in the bedroom," Erin replied vaguely. She didn't miss Katie's sigh as she rose from the sofa.

"I'd get it myself," Erin said. "But . . ." She gazed meaningfully at her bandage.

Katie cocked her head to one side. "Erin, it must be awfully uncomfortable sitting in that chair."

"It certainly is," Erin said fervently.

"Do you want to try walking?"

Erin closed her eyes. "I can't walk, Katie. Not yet. I'm much too weak."

"How do you know if you haven't tried?"

Erin's eyes opened, and she looked at Katie solemnly. "I have tried. Last night, after you guys went to bed." She put a hand to her forehead, as if the memory was painful. "I couldn't even stand. In fact, I fell. I had to crawl back to the sofa."

It was a great story. And Katie looked properly distressed. "Why didn't you yell for us?"

"I didn't want to wake you."

Katie bit her lip. "I'll get your magazine."

A moment later, she returned and handed it to her. Erin debated telling Katie this wasn't the magazine she wanted. But then she thought of something better. "This place is a mess," she murmured. "All that stuff on the coffee table . . ."

"Your makeup," Katie pointed out.

"And what's all that piled on the chair?"

"Your clothes from yesterday."

Erin smiled. "I just hate sitting around in a mess. Katie, would you mind straightening up? I'd do it, but . . ."

"I know, I know."

"And hand me my manicure kit, okay? And Katie, if you don't mind, could you go over to the lodge and get me a soda? I'm dying of thirst."

Katie nodded. But her fixed smile was definitely getting a little grim.

* * *

Katie saw Trina come into the lodge, and waved.

"What are you doing here?" she asked.

"Just taking a break," Trina said. "What are *you* doing here? Who's with Erin? You didn't leave her alone, did you?"

"I *had* to," Katie said. "She wanted me to get her something to drink."

She wasn't aware of how irritated she sounded until she saw the look of surprise on Trina's face.

"What's the matter?" Trina asked.

"Oh, Erin's driving me nuts. Katie, do this, Katie, do that. Turn on the TV, close the blinds. I'm getting her things, picking up her stuff. She hasn't stopped giving me orders since the second you guys left!"

If it was sympathy she was after, she realized immediately she wasn't going to get any from Trina.

"Katie, I know Erin can be a pain. But don't forget, it's your fault that she has to ask someone to do things for her."

"I know. But I'm starting to feel like she's taking advantage of how bad I feel. And you know what? I think she's enjoying herself!"

Trina looked shocked. "Katie, how can you

say that? Do you think Erin *wants* to be in a wheelchair?"

Katie shrugged. She wasn't sure what she thought. And anything she said was bound to result in a lecture from Trina.

Two girls, who looked a little older than they, were talking loudly, and Katie half listened to them.

"What are you wearing to the dance tonight?" one of them asked the other.

"What dance?"

"They have a dance here, upstairs, every Wednesday evening. With a real band."

Katie lost interest. Dances, even with real bands, never had much appeal to her. But Trina had been listening too.

"Did you hear that? About the dance?"

"What about it?" Katie asked. She'd never known Trina to show much interest in dances either.

"Do you realize how much Erin is going to hate missing that dance?" Trina demanded.

Katie shrugged again. "She can still go, even if she can't actually dance. I'll just wheel her here."

"No, you can't," Trina said. "Didn't you hear what that girl said? The dance is upstairs. There's no way you can get a wheelchair up a flight of stairs."

Suddenly, Katie felt very small. "You're right. Erin's going to be miserable when she hears about that dance. And it's all my fault she won't be going to it."

"Well, don't kick yourself," Trina said. "Just do what you said you were going to do. Try to make it up to her. Look, I'll stay with her the rest of the day. You can go do some skiing."

"No," Katie said. "I'm responsible for what happened. It's my job to take care of her. Like you said, I have to make it up to her."

She got Erin's drink. Then she squared her shoulders and headed back to the chalet. And silently, she resolved not to let Erin's demands get to her.

Chapter 7

By noon, Katie was having a rough time hanging on to her resolution. Erin had sent her to the gift shop at the lodge to get magazines, but when she returned with a whole stack, Erin didn't even bother to look at them. She ran a bath for Erin, and Erin complained that it was too hot. She'd gone back to the gift shop to get nail polish for Erin, but Erin didn't like the color she chose.

Katie was relieved when Trina, Sarah, and Megan returned from the slopes. At least there would be others around to deal with Erin's demands.

"We brought lunch so you wouldn't have to go to the lodge," Sarah announced.

Erin didn't seem to appreciate that. "Darn. I was looking forward to getting out of here. I feel like I'm in jail."

Megan spoke soothingly. "In a couple of hours you can go to the lodge for—what do you call it?"

"Après-ski," Erin snapped. "Really, Megan, can't you remember anything?"

Katie gave the others a significant look. Maybe now they'd realize what she'd been suffering through, alone here with Erin. For the zillionth time, she reminded herself what a drag it must be for Erin, trapped in a wheelchair. And that she, Katie, had put her there. Okay, maybe she deserved to be punished for what she'd done. But for how long?

"I've got a chicken sandwich here somewhere for you," Sarah said, digging into the bag.

Erin made a face. "Chicken. Yuck."

"I thought you liked chicken sandwiches," Trina said in surprise.

"That was yesterday. Today I'm in the mood for tuna salad."

Sarah grinned. "Guess what? I've got that too!"

That news didn't do anything to improve Erin's disposition. Sarah laid all the food out on the coffee table, and the girls gathered around.

"This is fun," Megan said in a voice that was almost too cheerful. "Like having a picnic."

"Yeah," Sarah chimed in. "It reminds me of Sunnyside, when we got goodie packages and had midnight snacks."

"Sunnyside," Erin echoed. "I wonder if I'll even be going back to Sunnyside this summer."

"Why wouldn't you?" Trina asked.

"Well, if I can't do any of the sports, what's the point?"

"Good grief," Sarah sputtered. "You'll be out of that wheelchair by *then!*"

"Who knows?" Erin said.

"That's strange," Megan said. "I have a friend back home who sprained her ankle. She was limping around the very next day."

Erin glared at her. "There are different kinds of sprained ankles," she snapped.

"Oh," Megan replied meekly.

Katie tried to get a normal conversation going. "How do you like skiing so far?" she asked Sarah.

Before Sarah could reply, Erin murmured, "Skiing. I wonder if I'll ever ski again?"

They ate the rest of the meal in silence.

* * *

Erin was bored. Yesterday had been fun. Not the accident, of course. But afterwards, when her ankle wasn't hurting so much, she'd actually enjoyed herself.

It was nice having people do everything for her. She could order them around, knowing they felt so sorry for her they'd do anything she told them.

But all that was becoming old now. Trina, Sarah, and Megan had gone back to the slopes. Erin was sick of magazines and TV, and she couldn't think of any errands to send Katie on, or any jobs she could do for her.

At least she had the après-ski time in the lodge to look forward to. That had been great yesterday—all that attention, all the people gathered around her. And Josh . . .

She frowned. Josh should have come by the chalet today to see how she was doing. He should have offered to give up skiing for the day to keep her company. Oh well, maybe she wasn't being fair. After all, he hardly knew her, and she hadn't had the opportunity to turn on the charm full blast or do any serious flirting. And he had other friends here, that whole high school group.

Her frown deepened. Some of those high school girls had been awfully cute. Why, right this minute, he was probably sitting on the lift with one of them.

She realized Katie was watching her with alarm. "Are you okay, Erin? You're making faces."

"It's nothing. Just a twinge in my ankle." She scrunched her eyes and gasped, as if a sudden pain had just shot through her. She was pleased to see Katie jump up.

"Do you want anything? Some aspirin, maybe?"

Erin considered the offer. "Could you bring me my makeup bag? And a mirror? That might help me feel better."

Katie rolled her eyes, but she did as she was told. She held the mirror while Erin applied makeup and thought about Josh. She wasn't about to let a sprained ankle ruin her chances for a holiday romance. Actually, her injury just might improve her chances. If she could get him really interested in her, surely he'd give up skiing to stay with her for the rest of the week.

One thing she knew for sure. She had to be at the lodge when he arrived there. She didn't want those high school girls having one more minute alone with him than necessary.

"How do I look?" she asked Katie.

"Fine."

"Are you sure? I'm not too pale?"

"No. In fact, for someone in a wheelchair, you look very healthy."

Erin looked at her suspiciously. But Katie's expression was totally innocent.

"You can take me to the lodge now," Erin announced.

Katie curtseyed. "Yes, ma'am." She collected their jackets, helped Erin on with hers, and pushed the chair toward the door. Erin stretched luxuriously as she rolled along. Maybe she should have waited until later, when Josh would already be in the lodge. It would be nice to make an entrance like this. She thought about ordering Katie to take her back. But she decided against it. Katie was showing some signs of annoyance with Erin. Erin didn't want to press her luck.

There weren't many people hanging out in the lodge yet. Erin surveyed the scene. Where should she sit? Where would Josh look first when he walked in?

"Put me over there," she directed Katie.

Katie pushed her to the corner, and Erin considered her position. She could see everything from there. But could she be seen?

"I've changed my mind. Put me over there."

Katie obliged. Now Erin was facing the entrance. This might look like she was lying in wait for him. It was too obvious. "Katie . . ."

There was no response. She twisted her head around. Katie wasn't there.

Then she spotted her at the bar. "Katie!"

"What?"

Erin hated to yell across the room. Princesses shouldn't have to yell. She beckoned.

Katie took her time walking back. "What do you want now?"

"Move me over there."

Katie put her hands on her hips. "Erin, you know you can move that thing yourself. You just have to push the wheels. There's nothing wrong with your arms."

Erin controlled her temper. "Gee, Katie, I didn't think I was asking so much." She couldn't resist reminding her one more time. "After all, it's because of you that I'm in this wheelchair."

Katie let out a long, weary sigh. "Erin, are you *ever* going to forgive me? I've given up skiing, I'm pushing you around, I'm running all your errands . . ."

Erin gazed sorrowfully at her ankle. "Do you think *that* makes up for *this?*"

Katie threw up her hands in resignation. "Okay, where do you want to go now?"

By the time skiers began to traipse in, Erin was settled. With a cup of hot chocolate in her hands, she sat by the fire and watched the door out of the corner of her eye. She saw Josh come in with his school friends. When he spotted Erin, he left them and came directly to her.

"How are you feeling today?" he asked.

"I'm better," Erin said. "Of course, it's been lonely, sitting around by myself." She gave him a smile and a sidelong look, hoping he'd get the hint.

Josh shook his head with regret. "You had crummy luck. It was great on the slopes today. The sun was out, and the snow was so smooth it was like skiing on air." As he started describing his runs down the hill, Erin had a difficult time keeping her smile in place. She wanted to move the topic of conversation away from skiing and on to *her.*

But before she could think of a way to do

that, two boys and a girl hurried over to them. Erin expected the same expressions of concern she'd received from them yesterday. But after a brief "hi" aimed in her general direction, they turned their attention to Josh.

"There's a free Ping-Pong table," the girl said. "Let's grab it before anyone else gets there."

"Great!" Josh said. He turned to Erin. "You want to—oh, I forgot. You can't."

"I don't mind just watching," Erin said quickly. That girl was awfully cute.

Josh shook his head. "The Ping-Pong tables are upstairs. You can't get up there in that wheelchair."

"C'mon, Josh," one of the boys urged. "Let's go."

"See ya later," Josh told Erin. And then he was gone.

The minute his back was to Erin, her smile disappeared. How humiliating! He'd rather play stupid Ping-Pong with his friends than be with her!

When she saw Peter and Michael walk into the lodge, she waved eagerly. They waved back. Then she realized they were accompanied by two girls. In disappointment, she watched them all move across the room.

Well, she knew one thing for sure. She wasn't going to be sitting here, alone and pathetic, when Josh came back down after his Ping-Pong game. She spotted Katie over by the bar, and she waved. But Katie didn't see her. Or maybe she was just pretending not to see her. She waved again. When that didn't produce any response, she put her hands on the wheels and pushed. The chair didn't budge. Katie must have put the brake on.

Now what was she going to do? she wondered in despair.

Katie looked up as her brothers and two giggling girls approached.

"Your friend's all alone over there," Michael pointed out.

"Then why don't you go keep her company?" Katie suggested sweetly. "You were the ones who wanted her to come."

"Uh, we're busy right now," Peter said. "Why is she still in the wheelchair anyway? She should be walking by now."

"She can't," Katie said.

"Sure she can," Michael argued. "Dad said it was just a minor sprain."

Katie glanced back at Erin. Unfortunately, Erin was looking directly at her. And she was flapping her hands in the air. Katie couldn't ignore her any longer. She walked over to her.

"It's about time!" Erin's face was red. "Didn't you see me waving?"

"What do you want?" Katie asked.

"I want to go back to the chalet. *Now!*"

"But it's almost time to eat," Katie said. "We're meeting Trina and Sarah and Megan here."

Erin's voice rose. "I don't care! I want to go back!"

"Okay, okay." Katie released the brake on the wheelchair and started back.

"What happened to your boyfriend?" Katie asked when they got outside.

"He's *not* my boyfriend," Erin hissed. "He left me to go play stupid Ping-Pong with his stupid friends."

"Oh, too bad." Katie remembered seeing the Ping-Pong tables upstairs. "Well, they can't play for very long."

"Why not?"

"Because they'll be setting up for the dance there."

There was a moment of silence from the wheelchair. "Dance? What dance?"

Katie gulped. How had *that* slipped out? She took her time fumbling for the key in her pocket and unlocking the chalet door.

"Tell me!" Erin demanded as Katie pushed her inside.

There was no way she could get around this. "There's a dance tonight at the lodge."

"I can't believe it!" Erin practically screamed. "A dance? Josh didn't even mention it!"

Katie tried to be kind. "Probably because he knew you couldn't dance. You wouldn't even be able to get up the stairs."

"He could have asked anyway!"

"Come on, Erin, don't make a big deal out of this."

"Why shouldn't I make a big deal!" Now Erin was shrieking. "It *is* a big deal! And it's all your fault, Katie! Now you've ruined my chance for a real holiday romance!"

"Stop it!" Katie shrieked right back. "I'm

sick of listening to you blame me! I said I was sorry!"

"What good is being sorry?" Erin yelled.

Katie couldn't stand one more minute of this. She let go of the wheelchair and ran out of the chalet. She was on her way back to the lodge when she saw Trina, Megan, and Sarah coming toward her.

"What's going on?" Megan asked. "I thought we were meeting at the lodge."

"She's driving me crazy!" Katie fumed.

"Calm down," Trina ordered. "Let's go back and talk this out with her." Together the girls started back. Then, right in front of the chalet, Trina stopped suddenly. She put a hand to her mouth.

"What's the matter?" Sarah asked.

In a hushed voice, Trina said, "Look."

They all turned toward the chalet window. The light was on, and the curtains were open, so they had a clear view of the interior. In unison, they all gasped.

There was Erin. Standing up. The girls watched in shock as she moved across the room.

"She can *walk,*" Sarah breathed.

"And she's hardly even limping," Trina said, her eyes wide in wonderment.

Katie felt like a fire had been lit inside her. She was *burning.* "Why that little phony! I'll bet she's been able to walk all along! It was an act, staying in that wheelchair and pretending she couldn't walk. She just wanted to make me feel worse than I already felt!"

"And get treated like a queen," Megan added. "You know she wouldn't want to give up all that attention."

Even Trina looked angry. "I'm going in there and having a little talk with her."

They all started toward the door. Then Katie clutched Trina's arm. "No, wait. I've got a better idea."

Trina cocked her head to one side. "Katie, you've got that look in your eyes. What kind of scheme are you up to?"

Quickly, Katie explained her plan to her friends. "It's perfect!" Megan exclaimed, and Sarah and Trina nodded in agreement.

"Wait here," Katie instructed. "I have one little detail to take care of, then I'll be right back."

She took off to the lodge. Upstairs, she

found Josh and some other kids at a Ping-Pong table.

"Um, excuse me, Josh. I need to talk to you for a minute." Katie smiled. "It's about Erin."

Chapter 8

Erin fidgeted in her wheelchair. Having those few minutes up when no one was in the chalet had felt good. Luckily, she had heard them talking outside, and managed to get back into the chair. She was sitting forlornly there by the time they walked in.

But they weren't even paying any attention to her.

"We don't have to dance," Sarah was saying to Megan. "We could just go and watch and listen to the music."

Megan grinned. "What if a boy asks us to dance?"

"We could consider it," Sarah replied.

"This is unbelievable!" Erin burst out. "Are you guys going to that dance? You're going to leave me sitting here all alone?"

"We might," Trina said.

Erin looked at her oddly. That didn't sound like Trina at all. "Where's Katie? I'm hungry."

"There's going to be food at the dance," Megan said.

"But what about me?" Erin wailed.

The door opened, and Katie came in. "Hi, guys," she said casually. "Oh, Erin, I ran into that guy, Josh."

Erin sniffed. "Who cares."

"He seemed kind of down," Katie said. "He told me he wanted you to be his date for the dance."

"He did?"

"Yeah. He said he wasn't much into dancing, but he'd wanted the two of you to just hang out there."

"He said that?"

"I told him he might as well ask another girl since there's no way you could get up those stairs."

"Thanks a lot," Erin muttered.

"Well, you can't, can you?" Katie scratched her head. "It's funny, though. He said he didn't want to ask anyone else. And he was hoping that by the time of the dance, you'd be able to walk."

"Katie, that's crazy," Trina said. "The dance starts in an hour. How could Erin be walking by then?"

"You know, I've heard that happens sometimes with sprained ankles," Megan commented. "One minute you're in a wheelchair, next minute you're walking around."

"I've never heard that," Erin said.

"Oh sure, it happens all the time," Sarah said.

Trina got up. "Well, I'm going to take a shower and get ready for this dance." Katie followed her. Megan and Sarah rose and went into the other bedroom.

Erin leaned back in her wheelchair and closed her eyes. She had some thinking to do.

"Let me see." Katie pushed against Trina.

"Shh," Trina murmured.

They were huddled by door in the bedroom, trying to see into the living room. They didn't dare open the door more than a tiny crack. Across the living room, they could see that Sarah and Megan's door was in the same position.

Katie heard a sharp intake of breath. "There she goes," Trina whispered.

Slowly, Erin rose from the wheelchair. She looked around furtively. Then, with barely a limp, she walked over to the table where her pocketbook lay.

The girls burst out of their rooms. "Erin, you can walk!" Trina exclaimed.

"It's a miracle!" Megan squealed.

Katie thought Erin's smile was a little uneasy. "Well, you *said* this happens with sprained ankles. And I was determined. I just can't disappoint Josh. I can't believe I can actually walk again."

Megan coughed, as if she was trying to choke back a giggle. "I read somewhere about a woman whose child was trapped under a car. She was so determined to save him, she was actually able to lift the car. Even though it was physically impossible."

"I guess it's what they call mind over matter," Sarah said.

"Exactly," Erin said eagerly. "I wanted to walk so bad that I could, even though it's physically impossible."

"Like Megan said, it's a miracle," Katie piped up.

Erin nodded. "I must really like Josh a lot. They say true love conquers all."

"I've heard that too," Trina noted.

"Let's go to the lodge," Sarah suggested. The girls put on their coats and started over there.

"You're walking so well, Erin," Katie commented. "It's truly amazing."

"Yes," Trina said, "especially considering that the doctor said he didn't know when you'd walk again. You'll have to call and tell him."

"Oh yes," Sarah agreed. "Why, Erin, you may have made medical history."

None of them could keep this up for too long. Megan was the first to start giggling. Sarah joined in. Then Katie and Trina cracked up.

"What's so funny?" Erin asked.

"You." Katie practically choked, she was laughing so hard. "Erin, you've been able to walk all along. We saw you through the window."

Erin went pale. Her mouth opened, but no words came out. She was trapped, and she knew it.

Katie expected her to give up and laugh along with them. But she didn't. Her eyes began to blaze, and she turned the fire on Katie.

"Then this was all a trick, huh? You never talked to Josh. You lied, just like you lied to get me on that hill. I can't believe you'd—"

"Erin!"

They all turned. Josh was coming toward them.

"Erin, you're walking! That's super!"

Erin's smile was stiff. "Uh, yes, well . . ."

"I guess Katie got my message to you."

Erin nodded. "Yes. She did."

Josh grinned. "C'mon, let's go."

"Just a second," Erin said. She limped over to Katie and pulled her aside. "I've got something to say to you."

Katie eyed her uncertainly. "What?"

"You're forgiven."

Katie nodded. "Thanks." And as she watched Josh take Erin's arm, she smiled in relief.

"At least Erin's vacation isn't completely ruined," she said to the others. "She can still have her romance."

"Which is more important to her than skiing anyway," Megan added.

"And *I* can get back on the slopes," Katie said happily. "You know, I didn't get to do a real run on that Monster—"

"No way!" Trina interrupted. "We just got one person out of that wheelchair, Katie."

"Yeah," Sarah said. "And if you think we're going to spend our vacations pushing you around, forget it!"

Katie pretended to be offended. "Boy, some friends you guys are."

Trina put her arm around her. "Good friends don't just push friends around in wheelchairs. They try to keep their friends from ending up in them."

Katie rolled her eyes, but she had to smile. Trina had a point. She wasn't quite ready for that slope anyway.

So once again, her brothers could claim they were better than she was. Maybe her brothers would always be better than she was, in some ways.

But there was no way they'd ever have better friends than she had.

MEET THE GIRLS FROM CABIN SIX IN

(#13) **BIG SISTER BLUES** 76551-9 ($2.95 US/$3.50 Can)
(#12) **THE TENNIS TRAP** 76184-X ($2.95 US/$3.50 Can)
(#11) **THE PROBLEM WITH PARENTS** 76183-1 ($2.95 US/$3.50 Can)
(#10) **ERIN AND THE MOVIE STAR** 76181-5 ($2.95 US/$3.50 Can)
(#9) **THE NEW-AND-IMPROVED SARAH** 76180-7 ($2.95 US/$3.50 Can)
(#8) **TOO MANY COUNSELORS** 75913-6 ($2.95 US/$3.50 Can)
(#7) **A WITCH IN CABIN SIX** 75912-8 ($2.95 US/$3.50 Can)
(#6) **KATIE STEALS THE SHOW** 75910-1 ($2.95 US/$3.50 Can)
(#5) **LOOKING FOR TROUBLE** 75909-8 ($2.95 US/$3.50 Can)
(#4) **NEW GIRL IN CABIN SIX** 75703-6 ($2.95 US/$3.50 Can)
(#3) **COLOR WAR!** 75702-8 ($2.50 US/$2.95 Can)
(#2) **CABIN SIX PLAYS CUPID** 75701-X ($2.50 US/$2.95 Can)
(#1) **NO BOYS ALLOWED!** 75700-1 ($2.50 US/$2.95 Can)
MY CAMP MEMORY BOOK 76081-9 ($5.95 US/$7.95 Can)

CAMP SUNNYSIDE FRIENDS SPECIAL:
CHRISTMAS REUNION 76270-6 ($2.95 US/$3.50 Can)

Buy these books at your local bookstore or use this coupon for ordering:

Mail to: Avon Books, Dept BP, Box 767, Rte 2, Dresden, TN 38225
Please send me the book(s) I have checked above.
☐ My check or money order—no cash or CODs please—for $________ is enclosed (please add $1.00 to cover postage and handling for each book ordered to a maximum of three dollars—Canadian residents add 7% GST).
☐ Charge my VISA/MC Acct# ________ Exp Date ________
Phone No ________ I am ordering a minimum of two books (please add postage and handling charge of $2.00 plus 50 cents per title after the first two books to a maximum of six dollars—Canadian residents add 7% GST). For faster service, call 1-800-762-0779. Residents of Tennessee, please call 1-800-633-1607. Prices and numbers are subject to change without notice. Please allow six to eight weeks for delivery.

Name ________

Address ________

City ________ State/Zip ________

SUN 0891

THE MAGIC CONTINUES... WITH LYNNE REID BANKS

THE SECRET OF THE INDIAN 71040-4/$3.50 U.S.

THE INDIAN IN THE CUPBOARD 60012-9/$3.50 U.S./$4.25 Can.

THE RETURN OF THE INDIAN 70284-3/$3.50 U.S.

And Don't Miss These Other Enchanting Books!

I, HOUDINI 70649-0/$3.50 U.S.

THE FAIRY REBEL 70650-4/$2.95 U.S.

Coming Soon

THE FARTHEST-AWAY MOUNTAIN

71303-9/$3.50 U.S.

Buy these books at your local bookstore or use this coupon for ordering:

Mail to: Avon Books, Dept BP, Box 767, Rte 2, Dresden, TN 38225
Please send me the book(s) I have checked above.
☐ My check or money order—no cash or CODs please—for $__________ is enclosed (please add $1.00 to cover postage and handling for each book ordered to a maximum of three dollars—Canadian residents add 7% GST).
☐ Charge my VISA/MC Acct# ________________ Exp Date __________
Phone No _______________ I am ordering a minimum of two books (please add postage and handling charge of $2.00 plus 50 cents per title after the first two books to a maximum of six dollars—Canadian residents add 7% GST). For faster service, call 1-800-762-0779. Residents of Tennessee, please call 1-800-633-1607. Prices and numbers are subject to change without notice. Please allow six to eight weeks for delivery.

Name ______________________________

Address ______________________________

City ________________ **State/Zip** ________________

LRB 1191